# Nash Walker: Feud on the Frontier

# Also by Patrick Lindsay

*Opening the Frontier: Spencer and Son*

**Latigo Series**

*Latigo's Choice: Taming the West*

*Latigo's Chance: Boomtown Gold*

*Latigo's Trouble: Meltdown in Leadville*

*Latigo's Pursuit: Answering the Call*

# Nash Walker: Feud on the Frontier

## Nash Walker
### Book 1

## Patrick Lindsay

WOLFPACK
PUBLISHING
— EST 2013 —

# Nash Walker: Feud on the Frontier

# Chapter 1
## *Home At the Still*

## Ashfork, Tennessee, 1873

I can't say I'm real proud of that still we've got out back, even though the moonshine I make is mighty fine. Actually, the still is down in the holler, mebbe half a mile from the house. It's nestled down there, alongside the crick that runs down out of the hills. Ma, she's been after me to shut down that still ever since I got back from the war, eight years ago.

Mostly, I listen to my ma. She's all I've got left now. I ran off to join the Army and fight for the South back in 1861, when I was only seventeen years old. The Army didn't ask a lot of questions about how old you were back then. They taken one look at the size of me, I guess, and decided I looked old enough.

I felt a whole lot older by the time that war was over, let me tell you. My pa and my brother didn't survive Shiloh, so I was the only one that marched home. Ma was mighty glad to see me, but I don't guess she was ever quite the same after she lost my pa and my brother. Now we just had each other.

Anyway, Ma wants me to shut down that still, and I've been meaning to, but a man's got to put food on the table, don't he? The scraggly few little vegetables in the garden and a couple of skinny chickens couldn't feed us. Plus, a little nip at a glass jar of shine puts me in a better mood from time to time. Folks say my disposition could use a bit of improvement now and then.

I don't exactly know what they mean by that, but I guess they're right. I'm mostly a peaceful man, I think. It takes a lot to get me riled up. Folks say that about me, too. "That Nash Walker," they say, "you don't want to get him riled up."

Ma seemed to have taken her time rising this morning. The sun was already up over the hills to the east, and she hadn't moved out of her room yet. Usually, she already had the coffee on by the time I'd rolled out. If it was a good day, she might even say I'm handsome, with my dark wavy hair and my brown eyes. I don't know about that, but it sounds nice. Right now, I was hungry. I wolfed down a couple biscuits and some gravy, then eased out the door of the shack and set down on the steps to put my boots on.

I moved along down the worn trail and along to the fencepost-and-rail corral I was always having to fix up in one place or the other, then stepped into what passed for a barn and got my saddle and the old Henry rifle Pa had left behind.

My horse Cisco was looking peaceful enough when I slipped the saddle on him. Cisco is a Tennessee walking horse with mebbe a little more mustang in him than what's usual for those walking horses. His gait ain't as smooth as some, but he's got speed and staying power. And he's got an attitude.

This morning, I gave him some oats and brushed him out a little, and it looked like we were going to get along. Sometimes he don't seem to like it when all six foot one and two hundred twenty pounds of me gets into the saddle. Once in a while, he gets his back up and we have a little go-around. He crow-hops around the corral and puts the evil eye on me. Today he took it peaceful enough when I mounted, so I moved him out of the corral and turned him down the trail toward the still.

The morning, when it's cool, is always my favorite time of day. It was moving on toward fall now, and the summer heat was easing up. The leaves were fluttering on the redbud and maple trees as we picked our way along a winding trail. I could hear the stream rushing by down below. That stream gave me the water for the 'shine.

Movement caught my eye as I rounded the bend. I slid down off Cisco, led him into the trees and tied him off, then slipped that old Henry out of the scabbard. Somebody had broken into the still! The door was partly open. I eased up to a tree trunk and got me a good look down below.

I gotta say, my jaw dropped a little at what I saw. There was a family by the name of Darnell in these parts, down the road and way back into the hills. They was in the same business as me. Mind you, my moonshine was better, but they made a decent bottle of hooch, and mostly we stayed out of each other's way. There was enough business to go around.

We'd had some disagreements and some fisticuffs

over the years, but it hadn't never come down to a shootin' war the way it had for a lot of folks in these parts. I hadn't even seen those boys around here for a good two years. We'd had us a little set-to back then, but I'd settled it with a hard right into Clem Darnell's jaw. Clem was the tough one.

I stared back down into the holler down below. Seth Darnell was the oldest and considered that he had the brains in the family, not that there was much of that to go around. Seth was carrying a bottle in each hand, and he was heading for a wagon. His little brother was sitting up front, ready to drive the wagon away. I shook my head. If they were fixing to carry away my corn or my sugar or somethin' like that, I'd know they just ran outta supplies. Why would they carry off the 'shine?

I braced the Henry up against a redbud tree and sighted in on the top end of that ugly black top-hat Seth always wore. When I squeezed off the Henry, that hat went flyin' up in the air, turned over once or twice, then landed in the bushes about fifteen feet away. Seth ran to the wagon faster than I thought he could move and dove in the back. His brother cracked the whip, and they took off. The wagon was bouncing so hard down that old rutted trail, I thought it would come apart. Seth was having him a rough ride there in the back.

The bottles of 'shine were still laying on the ground. I watched for a while without moving, but it was totally quiet down there now.

I slipped out of the trees and took a good look around for Clem, the other Darnell brother. He'd carried a grudge since I'd laid him out with a punch on his jaw a couple years ago. He had put up a good fight, I had to admit. He claimed I put him down with a lucky punch. I knew better. The only thing I'd learned to do in the Army besides how to march was how to fistfight. I already knew how to shoot a gun and swear when I got there.

Ma didn't hold with swearing, so I didn't do that anymore except in an emergency. Hitting my thumb with a hammer sets me off every now and then. The prizefighting skills I'd learned in the Army, though, had come in handy. My old sergeant, Buster, had taught me how to fight. He'd set up a ring when things slowed down, and we'd gone a round or two. I didn't expect to need them skills right now, though, on account the first two Darnell boys had skedaddled and I didn't see their brother Clem.

I scouted around when I reached the still. They had pried the lock off with a crowbar. I looked at the lock and shook my head. They'd busted it. The crowbar was still on the ground, so I would keep that. I carried the two jugs of 'shine back inside and checked around. The still was in good shape. Well, as good as it got, anyway. There were still twenty gallons of moonshine. They hadn't gotten any of it.

I came out of the still and nearly walked straight into a nasty punch in the face. I ducked just in time and Clem Darnell's big ham of a fist sailed over my head and into the door of the still. He commenced to doing some nasty cussin'. I lowered my shoulder and rammed it into his belly. I could hear the air whoosh out of him as he staggered back and fell on the grass.

I stood back and let him get up. He wouldn't have no call to say this was anything but fair and square. He doubled up those big hams of his and started circling around me. "I'm takin' your 'shine," he growled. "All of it."

I leaned over and spit in the grass. "I expect not," I told him. I remembered how he liked to put on a bull rush, and I could see him gathering himself up to do that now. When he charged, I stepped to one side and put out my foot. He went into the still door, head first and let out an impressive string of cuss words. I hoped Ma couldn't hear all that cussin' up at the house.

Clem spun away faster than I thought he could. I landed a glancing blow to the side of his head. He set himself and aimed a kick at my knee. I dodged the kick and swept his other leg. He landed with a heavy crash, then grabbed a handful of dirt and threw it at me as he struggled to get on his feet.

I turned my head as the dirt stung my cheek and the side of my neck, then stepped in and landed a hard short left to his eye. Clem fell back to the ground, his right eye swelling as blood trickled down his cheek.

He came off the ground with a roar, swinging left and right. I circled and ducked the blows. He had probably twenty pounds of muscle on me. Those swings could do some damage if he reached me. Finally, he swung until he ran outta air. His chest heaved, and he pawed at the blood that was getting in his eye.

I circled and waited. He was getting himself pretty tuckered out, but I figgered he had another bull rush in him. When it came, I stepped inside that heavy right hand and smashed him in the mouth with another hard left. Clem fell back to the ground, rolled over and spit out a tooth.

I waited. I never kick a man when he's down, and I wasn't gonna get down there and wrestle with him, neither. Clem wanted nothing more than to get those big arms wrapped around me and squash out the air.

Finally, he shook his head and slumped back to the ground. He stared at me with his good eye. "We jest wanted to take some of yer 'shine," he mumbled. "Nuthin' against you, Walker."

That didn't make no sense to me. "Why?" I barked. "You make your own hooch. Why didya want mine?"

Clem staggered to his feet and went looking for his horse. He fished around in his mouth and came out with another loose tooth. "Revenooers," he mumbled. "Revenooers shut us down an' busted up the still."

He found his horse and swung unsteadily aboard. "Watch yerself, Walker," he warned. "They'll be after you, too." Then he kicked his horse in the ribs and disappeared around the bend.

I went back inside and checked my supply again. Twenty gallons of hooch and a couple sacks of corn and sugar. I came back out and fixed up the door as best I could, then went to get Cisco. It was time to get back and check on Ma.

I didn't cotton much to those Darnell brothers, but I still had me a feelin' that Clem was telling me the truth about the revenooers. It puzzled me some because I'd not heard of those boys operating in these parts. Back east, in the Appalachian Mountains, the stills were thicker than flies, and those revenue boys were everywhere. I'd not seen 'em out here, just south of Nashville where I lived.

I thought about what I knew about the revenue agents. Back east, they found themselves on the wrong end of a shotgun sometimes, but they kept comin' and they were gettin' the best of things. They liked to get themselves a local boy who would give up news on where to find the stills and such. I'd not heard of any such things around here, but Ashfork was tiny. Then again though, they'd heard about the Darnell's still, some way.

I reached the shack and turned into the corral. I rubbed Cisco down and gave him a bait of grub, then headed for the shack. I stopped to wipe my boots off real good. Ma was particular about that. I pushed through the door.

"Ma!" I shouted. She didn't answer, which wasn't like her. She should be up and cooking me a breakfast by now. I shouted again. Still nothing.

I went into the kitchen. I expect I still couldn't quite believe she wasn't out there frying up the eggs and bacon. Everything was just the way it'd looked when I left to check the still this morning.

I stopped outside her door and hollered. When she didn't answer, I got me a bad feeling all over. I knocked on the door and still heard nothing. That left me wondering what to do next. If I went in there and there was nuthin' wrong, she might just start looking for that hickory switch she'd used on me when I was a kid.

Still, I had to know. I pushed the door open and saw her laying there real peaceful under the covers. She didn't have much color in her face, though. I went over and laid a hand on her forehead. She was cold to the touch.

I backed up and plopped down in her old rocking chair across the room and stared at the floor. She must have gone during the night, real peaceful. I'd heard nothing. For a long time, I sat there and stared at nothing, then got up and moved out to the yard, looking for my shovel. I had things to do and even more things to think about.

\* \* \*

I buried Ma under the apple tree near the garden. She said she had planted it when her and Pa moved into the place, and it was her favorite. I took off my hat and said a few words over her as best I could, reading from the Good Book.

After that was done, I sat on the front steps for a long time, trying to figure out where I would go. I knew for sure I was leaving here. Ma was the only thing that had kept me here this long. I just didn't know where I wanted to go. Lots of folks were going west, but I wasn't too sure about that.

Goin' north wasn't gonna happen. I had no hard feelings after the war, but that didn't sound like a place for a southern boy like me. That left the south. Texas? I'd heard some good things, but I didn't even know how to get there.

I sighed and moved into the house. Packing things up didn't take too long. I still had the duffel bag I'd used when I marched off to war, and it didn't take long to fill it. I threw in my clothes and the coffee pot, along with some coffee and a little food. And the Good Book. Ma would've been proud of me for that.

I carried the duffel bag out to the corral, then hitched Cisco and Ma's old horse on to the wagon. I tossed the bag in back and made one last trip to the still. The twenty jugs of 'shine went straight into the wagon when I got there. Mebbe I could make a few dollars with those. I only had five dollars in my pocket.

I took one last trip into the still and looked around. I thought about taking the axe to it. I'd tossed that axe and a shovel into the wagon. I decided against chopping it all up, but I put the axe to work on the tub I'd used for the corn mash. That could make firewood. If the revenooers came, maybe they would waste a lot of time waiting for me to show up.

I climbed back into the wagon and picked up the reins, ready to cluck at Cisco. Then I heard the clip-clop of hooves coming down the trail. I looked up to see a stranger coming my way, maybe my age or a little younger. Dark, wavy hair like mine, but he was shorter by a couple inches.

When he got close, I decided he would be a couple years younger. Salty, though. He'd seen some things. I could tell by the eyes. His shoulders were broad and packed heavy with muscles. He pulled up and nodded peacefully enough. He tipped his cap.

"Howdy," was all he said.

I answered the same and waited. He nudged his horse forward, keeping his hands in view. He stopped next to Cisco and nodded. "Nice hoss," he told me.

I said nothin' and he moved on to take a look in the wagon. He let out a low whistle. "I'll buy some of that off ya," he offered. "Buck fifty each, two gallons?" He nodded at his saddlebags. "Can't carry no more."

"Done." I climbed off the wagon and gave him the jugs. He gave me the money. "Levi," he said, "Levi Noone." He gave me a sideways look. "Noone. My real name is Nathan Bedford Noone, like Nathan Bedford Forrest, but I go by Levi."

"Rode with General Forrest," I said. I stuck out my paw. "Nash. Nash Walker."

He gave my hand a powerful squeeze and looked back into the wagon. "Where ya goin', Nash Walker?"

I stuffed the money into my pocket and shrugged. "I don't rightly know," I admitted. "Somewhere south. Texas, mebbe. Not sure yet." I glanced at the guns he carried. He had a Henry rifle, but newer than mine. He had a sidearm too—it looked like a Colt Model 1860 in a holster on his hip.

Levi Noone's eyes lit up when I said Texas. "I'm from Texas," he blurted. "Goin' back there now. You in need of a saddle partner?"

# Chapter 2
## *Southward Bound*

"Texas. Huh." I backed up about three steps and sat down in the doorway of the still. I'd been thinking about Texas, but thinking about it and doing it are two different things. My brain couldn't seem to get hold of it right away. I tried turning it around in my head a few times. You could almost hear the gears grinding.

Levi Noone studied me for a while. "You got a girl here or somethin'?"

I shook my head.

"Kinfolks?"

"Not anymore." I shook my head.

Noone looked around. He stepped over and stuck his head inside the still. "Well," he mumbled, "I kin see how you're havin' trouble leaving all this behind."

Well, I've gotta admit, that was pretty funny. I let out a chuckle or two, then had a good belly laugh. "When are you gonna leave for Texas?" I asked.

Levi Noone patted his saddlebag. "I've got me some 'shine. I expect now is as good a time as any."

I stood and walked over to my horse. "I've already

got my gear packed," I told him. "Just let me stop by the shack and take one more look around." I stared into the back of the wagon, then took out one bottle of 'shine and carried it back inside the still.

"Even revenooers get thirsty sometimes," I told Levi. I picked up the firewood I had chopped and looked around. The big copper pot was the only thing that was worth much, and I couldn't carry that all the way to Texas. I shrugged and left it where it was. Maybe somebody would find the pot and use it.

I climbed back up into the wagon. "We must be going south if we're headed for Texas," I said. "I've got a good idea where we can stop on the way, and I can sell the 'shine. It don't hurt to have a little extra money in my pocket."

**\* \* \***

We stopped at a trading post about twenty miles down the trail. Levi had told me we would follow the Cumberland River to the Tennessee River, then stop in Jackson, Tennessee, for whatever supplies we needed.

Levi pulled up alongside the wagon after about an hour on the trail and peered into the back. "You gonna try to keep that wagon after you sell the 'shine?" he asked.

I shook my head. "I don't expect I wanna bounce down the trails all the way to Texas. I'll sell it or jest leave it behind in Jackson."

Levi nodded and moved past to take the lead. "Probably be too invitin' for the bandits along the trail, anyway."

I clucked at the horses to move back up beside Levi.

"You expecting many bandits on the way?" I glanced down at my old Henry, riding in the seat beside me.

Levi leaned over and spit on the side of the trail. "I reckon. There's always a few bad'uns tryin' to lighten my wallet on the way. We kin discourage 'em." He looked over at the Henry. "You any good with that thang?"

I grinned and nodded. "Just try me. I can hit 'most anything I aim at."

Levi thought that one over. "Good. You got a sidearm?" He patted the Army Colt in the holster at his side. "Got yerself a pistol?"

"Nope. Never had much use for one since the war."

"Hmmm," Levi said. "Mebbe we can do somethin' about that." He drummed his heels into his horse's ribs and took the lead again. As he passed, I noticed a shotgun tied down on his horse. I had an idea now of how he discouraged bandits on this trail.

\* \* \*

We reached Jackson in a few days. We had to pull up and let a train pass in front of us, making an infernal noise. I hadn't seen one since the war, and I hadn't missed 'em none. Cisco got skittish and took to dancing sideways. I got down and held his muzzle to calm him down some.

I stopped at the blacksmith on Main Street to get my horse shoed while Levi proceeded to the first saloon he could find. Not that he hadn't lowered the 'shine level in one of them jars considerably. I guess a man needs a change ever' now and then to what he's drinking.

I stopped off at the general store to get us some supplies, then joined Levi in the saloon for a good, cold beer. I'd missed that, I gotta say. We split a pitcher.

"Wanna stay in a boarding house in town?" he asked.

I shook my head. "Ain't really got the money for it, and I'd just as soon sleep on the ground as in one of them lumpy beds. No tellin' who was in there before me."

Levi polished off the pitcher, stood up, and waved at me. "Just as well. Let's do somethin' about that extra moonshine in the wagon." He led me down the street, then pulled into an alley behind a trading post. He disappeared into the back of the place, then came out a few minutes later with a guy who came over to inspect the goods.

This guy was maybe twice my age and didn't look like he'd missed many meals lately. He picked up a bottle and held it up to the light, then popped the lid and took himself a taste. He grinned and nodded up and down.

"I'll give ye six bits for each," he thundered.

"Done!" I shook his hand and started handing out the bottles. Levi stopped me when I got to the last two. "This here trail is long and hard," he observed. "A man could use some comfort now and then." He gave me three dollars and kept the last two for himself.

The trading post owner threw in an extra two dollars for my beat-up old wagon, and I took it in a hurry. I stuffed my money in my pocket. I would look at it later. That was more money than I'd had in one place, ever.

Levi stopped off at the general store on our way out

of town. I waited outside and lounged against the hitching rail, watching the wagons, horses, and folks parading up and down the street. I hadn't been in a town this big in a long time.

Jackson had some pretty ladies. I noticed that right away. I don't know what they saw when they took a look at me, though. I'm a big, long man with dark hair. My ma said I have a firm chin. I expect that's because it had soaked up some punches. Ma also said I was handsome, but she was my ma. You've got to allow for that. My broad shoulders, I figure I got from Pa.

Anyway, I just minded my own business until Levi came out and mounted up. He led the way out of town for about two miles, then pulled off on a little side trail and followed that to a small clearing. There was a circle of rocks in the middle. I knew he must have camped here before. We got down and set up camp.

When we'd laid out our blankets and got some supplies out of the saddlebags for dinner, Levi came over and handed me something wrapped in paper. I opened it and found a new leather holster. I stared at him.

"You've got to git familiar with a sidearm if you're goin' to Texas," he informed me. "That holster is a gift."

"I ain't got a pistol," I reminded him.

"Let's do something about that." He dove back into his saddlebags and came out with another 1860 Army Colt. He handed it to me. "It's an extra," he explained. "The guy that used to own it has no use for it anymore. Gimme back my three dollars for those two jugs and we'll just call it even."

I took the 1860 Army Colt, looked down the barrel, gave the cylinder a spin, and put it in the holster. I pulled my old Army gun belt from my saddlebag, slipped the holster on it, and strapped it on. "Thanks," I told him.

It was Levi's turn to look surprised at the way I'd handled the weapon. "You've used one of those before. Army?"

I nodded.

"Well," Levi drawled, "you was either an officer or in the cavalry. Which was it?"

"Cavalry. Shiloh was ugly. Lost my pa and my brother. Nathan Bedford Forrest was lookin' for volunteers for the cavalry. I didn't figure it could be worse than being a foot soldier."

"Good," he said. "That will give us a head start on your training. Can you draw it quick and fire?"

"Nope," I said. "Never tried. I can aim it and hit what I'm aimin' at, at least I could. Never did none of that quick-draw stuff, though. Mainly just had to work at steadying it down while my horse was running."

Levi went to my old horse that was now a packhorse and took out two cans of beans and a cooking pot from the pack. He opened the beans with his knife and emptied them into the pot. "That'll be dinner," he announced, pointing at the pot. He took the empty cans, walked down the trail, and put them on a rock.

"Lessons start right now," he told me.

"Hold on," I said. "What are you gonna do for a spare? Don't you need this gun?"

Levi shook his head. "First of all, you backin' me up on a play is better than me digging around in my bags, trying to find another gun if I need one. Second, I hear Colt is comin' out with a new gun any time now that'll be way better than this one. They say it will fire six cartridges. No powder and ball to reload. I'm gonna get one as soon as I can. Might save my hide."

My brain was still soaking that up. "So...you're saying that you won't have to pour in the powder and ball and cap an' such in each chamber? Just stick a cartridge in each chamber when you reload and go?"

"Yup." Levi's eyes were downright shining. "Just open the cylinder, put in six cartridges, close up the cylinder, thumb 'er back and fire six times. Reloading is as easy as can be."

"Huh!" I made a note in my brain to get me one of those just as soon as I could. Meanwhile, he was telling me I had to learn how to use this one better. I pulled out the Army Colt, held it with two hands, sighted, and pulled the trigger. One can flew up in the air.

"Okay," Levi said slowly, looking at the can. "You can hit what you're aimin' at, but you ain't gonna have time to stand like somebody in one of them picture books, all posed and pretty and such. You got to shoot sooner."

We went through about ten or twelve shots with me learning to draw, point, and shoot. Levi taught me to take enough time to be sure I'd cleared the holster, to aim and shoot with one hand, not with two hands on the gun. After the first four or five shots with one hand, I started to hit the cans. Then I worked on drawing and shooting a little faster.

Levi called time after I'd emptied the Colt twice. I told him I couldn't afford to pay for no more ammo just then. While I reloaded, he told me we would just practice a little more every day or two.

"You've been in the war," he told me, "so I don't have to tell you it's all different when somebody is shootin' back. You look pretty natural and quick gettin' that gun out. You'll get faster just with the practice. Make sure you take enough time to make the bullet count."

Levi turned around and walked to the circle of rocks to build a fire. "I figure I'm doin' you a favor with these lessons, so you git to cook the dinner."

* * *

We took the trail south out of Jackson, winding through some rolling hills and thick forests. There were small towns here and there, but we didn't stop. The second day out, the hills and forests started to open up into some farmland.

We moved into some open land, leaving the trees behinds us. By the third day, we hadn't seen a stream for a while, but a farmer let us pump some water for the canteens and the horses. The guy watched us for a while, saying nothing. Levi took a swig and glanced over at him.

"We in Mississippi yet?"

"Yup." He scratched his chin and pointed back behind us. "You'uns crossed over mebbe three miles back down the trail."

We mounted up and moved on, pushing through Mississippi and into the state of Louisiana over the next few days. It got swampier the farther we went, and Levi warned me about alligators if I got too close to the water. I kept a sharp eye out. I hadn't come this far to turn into gator meat.

The fishing was good in Louisiana. We rigged up a couple of lines and hooks and hauled in plenty of bass for fresh food. After a few days, though, I was kind of fished out and decided to go deer hunting, first chance I got. Along about the ninth day on the trail, we crossed into Texas, and the land opened up and stretched out before us. I was surprised at the pine trees.

We set up camp at evening time on our first day in Texas. I unloaded my gear, stared around me at the pine trees and fields, then I picked up my Henry rifle.

"Where ya going, pilgrim?"

I stared at Levi. "Pilgrim? Now I'm a pilgrim?"

"Yore in Texas now," he reminded me.

I rolled my eyes and swung aboard Cisco. "I've got me a hankering for some deer meat," I told him. "I've et enough fish to grow some gills and I need some red meat."

Levi pushed himself off his bedroll and moved to his horse. "I'll ride along," he offered. "I want another look at what you can do with that Henry."

We walked the horses through the pine trees. I kept the rifle handy and pulled a spyglass from my saddle-bag. We reached the edge of the pine trees, and I saw what I was looking for, across a field at the edge of more pine trees. A four-point buck! I passed the spyglass to Levi.

"Whaddya think?" I whispered. "Three hunnerd yards?"

Levi passed the spyglass back and nodded. "At least. Mebbe three-fifty."

I eased down off Cisco, handed the reins to Levi, and crept to the edge of the pasture. I braced the Henry up against a pine tree, sighted down the barrel, held my breath and squeezed 'er off. The buck jumped once, fell to the ground and kicked a time or two. I heard a low whistle behind me.

"I guess I won't call you a pilgrim no more," Levi mumbled.

I field-dressed the buck, and we had venison for dinner. I got nothing against fresh fish, but this was what I wanted. We both leaned back on our bedrolls, up against our saddles, and let dinner hit bottom.

"How do you go about that bounty huntin', anyway?" I asked after a while. "I mean, how do you decide who to look for and where to look for him and such?"

I couldn't see Levi shrug over there in the dark, but I know he did. "Mostly, I look at the posters they've got up in the sheriff's office in a bunch of towns. Not in the big cities—there's too many guys doing the same thing there. I go to some of the smaller towns."

"Then how do you start looking for them?" I asked. "You don't know how old those posters are. They could've gone clear to California, for all you know."

"That's true," he agreed. "Sometimes the sheriff will tell me something that helps, sometimes not. I expect some of those boys want the bounty for themselves. Saloons are a good place to ask around, and maybe the general store or blacksmith. If I think I've got a lead on one of 'em, I just keep asking and riding, lookin' to see if the trail gets warmer."

I folded my hands behind my head and stared up at the stars, wondering again what I would do to make some money in Texas. I didn't expect there would be much call for moonshine and trapping down here. Levi interrupted my thoughts.

"Why are you asking? You want to join me on some

bounty hunts? I could mebbe use somebody watching my back."

I half-raised up on one elbow and looked across the camp at him. "Maybe," I said. "I don't have any other plan for what to do when we get to where you're going. Where is that, anyway? Austin?"

"Yep, near Austin," he said. "I'd be glad to have you along with me. We could catch twice as many outlaws and share the money. You got to practice a little more with that pistol, though. When you catch somebody in a saloon or in the middle of town, there can be some close-up shootin' sometimes. We can work on it a little more in the morning."

* * *

We got a bit of a late start the next morning, on account of some target practice. Levi allowed that I was getting pretty good. *Mighty quick and passing accurate* is what he said. I was glad of that, because we were goin' through a lot of ammo.

It was nigh onto noon, and we were moving out of the pine trees and into some open land with a few rocky formations here and there when we saw some dust being kicked up on the trail ahead of us. Levi reined in his horse, and I did the same.

"Four or five comin' this way, I'd guess," Levi said. "And they don't much mind lettin' folks know they're coming. He stirred around in his saddle uneasily and looked around us. He pointed toward a nest of boulders off to the side.

"Let's head for them rocks," he said. He looked over

his shoulder. "Keep that Henry where you can get at it," he warned.

# Chapter 3
## *Welcome to Texas*

The pack horse was slowing me down some, and the closer those boys got to us, the more I started thinking' they weren't here to invite us to a Sunday picnic. They saw us headed for the rocks and tried to beat us there, fanning out to flank us. I levered the Henry and snapped a shot that slowed 'em down. Levi grinned at me and led the way into the rock formation.

They slowed to spread into a half-circle, sizing up the situation. I counted five of them against just the two of us. I looked around behind me. There was some open ground, front and back, for maybe sixty to a hundred yards. Beyond that, there were scattered pine trees all around. They retreated behind some trees, no doubt sizing things up.

"Five of us an' two of you," somebody hollered. I squinted into the trees. There was a guy in a red shirt with a big belly over there. He had his hands cupped, and I figured him for the one doing the talking.

"I can count too," Levi shouted back. Things got quiet for a while.

The boulders we'd crouched behind were maybe waist high, so they gave some shelter to Levi and me, but those boys could shoot our horses if they wanted to and leave us in a bad way. They could also sneak around behind us after dark and open fire. I didn't want to think about bullets ricocheting off these rocks.

"Toss out yore money belts and whatever valuables you got. We'll let you move on," the same voice shouted. I snorted out loud. These boys were playing for keeps, I knew that much. There would be no moving on for us if they got their way.

We hunkered down and said nothing. A moment later, a rifle shot rang out from the trees, and the packhorse went down. Levi swore under his breath and looked over at me. "Time for you to show 'em what you can do with that Henry," he muttered.

I risked a glance over the rocks and thought that one over. Levi seemed to know what I was thinking. It was them or us. This was for keeps.

"Busted leg or arm won't do it," he growled. "I've seen the like of these varmints before. You're gonna have to take at least one of 'em out. I'd start with that big-bellied loudmouth that's been yellin' at us. Can you get a bead on him?"

I laid the Henry across the rocks and took a long look, then nodded at Levi. Big Belly had leaned out from behind a tree to yell at us some more. I centered the sights on his chest, took a long breath, held it, and squeezed off the shot. He pitched over backward and lay there beside a big pine tree. There was a long, stunned silence over there, then they started scrambling back. I sighted the Henry again, focusing this time on a leg sticking out from behind a tree. The second shot left a guy rolling on the ground, grabbing his leg.

I left off and waited, watching as they scrambled for their horses and rode out. After a few minutes, we were sure they had left. I stood and stared across the field. It looked like the wounded man had made it to his horse. They had left the dead man behind.

Levi moved around to check the packhorse, and I heard him swearing under his breath again. "They got the hooch," he explained. "Whole gallon of it gone."

I was still staring across the field. Levi moved up beside me and patted my shoulder. "Not much different from the war, really," he said. "Mebbe they'd have left us alive, but I don't think so. They don't wanna be lookin' over their shoulders for us for the rest of time. They'd likely have shot us and taken everything we've got if we'd let 'em."

We stripped the pack from the dead horse and spread it between our two horses as best we could. They could go for a short way with the extra load. Levi stared at the overhead sun. "We've still got time to make it to Marshall," he said, "if we move right out."

I looked back over at the man I'd shot. "What about him?" I asked. "They just left him there. We ain't got a shovel," I mumbled to myself.

Levi swung aboard his horse and stared across the pasture. "You got any good words to say over him if'n we bury him?" he asked. "Anything to say at all except he's dead for sure?"

I shook my head.

"Me neither," he said. I mounted up on Cisco, rode across the field, and found a few rocks to pile on top of him. Levi stood and watched while I rode back.

"Maybe the buzzards won't get him, anyway," I said. Then I turned Cisco and followed Levi on the trail to Marshall. It would be the first town of any size we'd been to in a couple of weeks. I looked back at the circle of rocks where we'd taken shelter just a little while ago. What I'd heard about Texas bandits was turnin' out to be true, so far anyway. We would have to keep our eyes peeled.

**\* \* \***

Victoria Ridley stood in front of a building on Seventh Street in Georgetown, Texas, and stared at it doubtfully. The sign across the front of the building said *Temperance Hall.* The building itself seemed to be in pretty good shape. It was a dull-colored stucco building, but it looked solid enough. Victoria knew they'd held a Bible study in here last night. Tonight, they would be opening a vaudeville show in this same building. She shook her head and wondered how many of the same people would show up to the vaudeville show from the Bible study crowd.

Seventh Street looked to be pretty busy. Maybe if they put a good sign out front, it would help draw a crowd. People passing through town to do some business might notice the sign and come back to see the show. Georgetown had only about eight hundred people in the town, so they would need some folks coming from the farms and ranches in the area to keep up a good crowd.

She studied the building again. It wasn't much, but they could make it work. The roof looked a little uneven in spots, but the owners had assured the acting company it didn't leak. She pushed open the doors and walked in. Her spirits lifted a little as she looked around.

There were chairs spread around the room, and they mostly lined up to form even rows. There was a balcony behind her with several rows of wooden chairs stretched across the width of the building. She was guessing this place could hold a hundred people or more. If they could fill it up three nights a week, maybe the show would last here for a month or two. That would be nice. Maybe they could charge twenty-five cents apiece. Kids would get in for free.

The last three months had seen them moving from town to town in Louisiana and East Texas. Victoria's family had a small ranch near here, but she hadn't been there for a visit yet. They still couldn't understand why she would travel around so much, singing and doing a comedy sketch, but she'd probably never be able to explain it. At age twenty-three, she needed something more than the family ranch. She had been singing in church and in the village square since she was four years old.

Victoria climbed the two steps to the stage and looked around. She shouted *Hey!* to test the acoustics and wasn't disappointed with the echo she got in return. She took a quick look through the door at the side of the stage. There wasn't much room back there, but they could gather and enter the stage from the side.

With one more look around, she climbed down off the stage and left the hall. Maybe they could do well enough here to book a bigger place down the road in Austin. That would be nice. With a little luck, maybe they could play San Francisco someday. Well, she had to admit that would take more than a little luck. Still, maybe Georgetown was a good start.

* * *

Marshall, Texas, was a lot bigger than I'd thought. It seemed almost as big as Nashville and maybe busier. For a moonshiner and trapper from Tennessee, this place was about as busy as I could handle.

We'd left the horses at a livery stable, and now I was staring at a building on the busiest street in town. Levi was pushing at my elbow.

"C'mon man, you sold all that 'shine. You've got to spend a little and live it up."

"Capitol Hotel." That was all I managed to say. I'd stayed at a boardinghouse a time or two, but never a hotel. I shuffled my feet uncomfortably and didn't move. Levi sighed impatiently.

"You've done had a shave at the barbershop and a bath out back. What else do you want? You want one of them in-vi-ta-tions? You won't scare the ladies now."

I stared down at my knees, where Ma had patched several tears in my pants. Levi heaved another huge sigh. "We'll git you another pair of britches before we eat dinner. I promise. First, we've got to get us a room." He gave me one more little shove, and I went in to register.

When we sat down to eat dinner later on, I was kinda glad for all the times Ma had slapped my hands and told me to eat my food proper. My brother and me had mainly wanted to get the food to our mouths as fast as possible, but thanks to Ma, I knew my way around with a knife and fork. This food was mighty good after two weeks on the trail, but I was careful not to bolt it down.

I started thinking I'd told Levi a lot about me, and he'd seen where I came from, but I didn't know much about him.

"You come from around here?" I finally asked. He stopped hoisting the food to his mouth long enough to nod.

"'Bout twenny miles south and west of here," he agreed. "Mostly east. Had us a little hard-scrabble farm with four or five cows, some pigs and chickens, and a garden. Weren't much there for the four of us." He stopped to wave for another beer. "My sister, she ran off back east when I wasn't more'n seventeen. I get a letter from her every now and then."

That didn't sound a lot different from how I'd grown up, except maybe for the moonshine. "You did some farming, then?"

He shrugged. "A little. Didn't much like scratching in the ground. I did a lot of huntin' in these trees and thickets around here. Got to be a dead shot, bringin' home deer meat. In hard times, squirrels, and opossum. Lots of them a little east, over toward Louisiana where it can get kinda swampy."

"War?" I asked. "Maybe you was a little young for the war."

"Yep." He nodded. "I was young, but they didn't care much. I ran off and signed up when I was seventeen, just about a year before it was all over." He stopped and took a pull of his beer. "I was with General Hood's boys, retreating through Tennessee. Got captured before Sherman got to Atlanta. Spent six months in a prison camp."

He seemed a little played out on talking right then, so we finished our steaks, then dug into some apple pie and coffee. I was wondering why I hadn't had any hotel dining room food before. This was like heaven.

"When I came home from that prison camp, I found my folks were dead," he said suddenly. "Malaria, they tell me. They'd done been buried about a month before, and folks didn't know how to reach me."

He stopped talking and pushed his pie around the plate with his fork. I waited. "Two guys had robbed the place, right after my folks died," he growled. "Ran off the pigs and chickens, drove the cows down the road and sold 'em to people forming up a drive to Kansas." He stared at the wall. "I found out they were wanted. Both of 'em. Wanted for murder."

"That's how you became a bounty hunter," I guessed.

He nodded. "Yep. Fifty-dollar reward for both of 'em. Dead or alive. I knew how to track and shoot. It weren't really that hard."

I waited, trying to decide whether to ask him the question I had in mind. He guessed what I was thinking and spared my asking.

"Only one of 'em was alive when I brought 'em in. He didn't last long, though. I collected my money, bought some cows, and merged 'em in with a drive to Kansas. Made me some good money, but I didn't care for smackin' the back of a horse all the way to Kansas. Came home and went back to bounty huntin'. Suits me better."

I thought that one over. "What's the law like down here?" I asked. "Sheriffs and such, I guess."

He nodded. "Yep, counties got sheriffs. Some of 'em are pretty good. State law, though, that's a pretty mixed bunch. We got the Texas State Police, but we don't think much of 'em in these parts. I don't expect they'll last long. Some of 'em are just as crooked as the outlaws. Texas Rangers have been around a while, an' they're better. A lot of the Rangers are watching the borders and such. They're not around here so much. I steer clear of all of 'em, anyway."

"You boys want some more pie?" I jumped a little— I hadn't seen anybody comin' up behind me. The waitress was younger than me, but pretty cute, I gotta say. "Uh...yeah, maybe another slice," I mumbled. She smiled and left.

The stormy look on Levi's face went away, and he started to chuckle. "I think she's maybe got her cap set for you," he drawled. "And yore face is all red and everything."

I just ignored him. Sometimes that's all you can do. I started thinking, though, that if there were more girls like her in these parts, maybe the move to Texas was a good idea. Even with the bandits and outlaws and such.

* * *

Next morning, we were loaded up and moving at first light. Levi said the business was better, and he knew more about the area down south of here, closer to Austin. He wanted to check in with the sheriff in Georgetown, just north of Austin, he said. This was all still new to me. I just saddled up and followed him out of town.

* * *

Victoria enjoyed sitting on a bench across the street from the Temperance Hall to watch the crowd when they left the show. Her last number was fifteen minutes before the end of the performances, so she had plenty of time to get out of costume and watch the people.

This evening, they were chattering and laughing at the last comedy sketch, and seemed to be in high spirits. She grinned as she remembered the response she'd gotten to singing *Clementine* and *Home on the Range*. Applause like that was the reason she did this.

When the crowd had dispersed, she went back inside to collect her things and then joined a few others in the walk back to the boardinghouse where they were staying while in town. They had a break for the next week because the Temperance Hall was booked for town meetings. When she reached her room at the boardinghouse, Victoria sat on her bed and thought about what she needed to do. She needed to visit home. She actually felt a little guilty she hadn't done that yet.

The family ranch was about ten miles the other side of Taylor, Texas, which made it a long one-day ride from Georgetown. Her father would make a fuss about her traveling it alone, but the main trail would be safe enough, and the family would be delighted to see her.

Following breakfast the next morning, Victoria walked down the street to the Georgetown post office. She kept her mother informed about the towns they would be visiting, and it wasn't unusual to find a letter waiting in her name at the post office. She found one this morning when she checked.

Moving across the street to the diner, Victoria ordered another cup of coffee and settled in to read the letter. Things at home hadn't been going well, she knew that. It was probably why she had put off a visit. The family ranch was a small one, though the pastureland was good, and they had an abundant source of water with a stream flowing across the land.

The stream was actually part of the problem. A much bigger outfit—a big ranch named *The Rolling R*— needed that water and coveted the pastureland as well. Things hadn't turned into a shooting war, but if they did, her family would be forced off the land.

The letter started out cheerily, which was her mother's nature. News about the community and crop conditions took up the first page. From there, though, her mother's worries started to show. Victoria continues reading.

"I'm worried about your father. He's out with the cows and crops from dusk till dawn, and your brother Rusty is with him every day. He's thought about putting up fences where the land borders Rolling R property— the Erskine ranch, but they probably wouldn't last. Your father takes his rifle with him as always, but tells Rusty he's too young at sixteen to go armed. I worry about them every day. We have one ranch hand now. He's a good man, but he wouldn't be much help against the Rolling R hands. Your father doesn't want to hear about selling the land."

The letter finished with a little more news and her mother saying how much she hoped Victoria would come for a visit. Victoria finished her coffee and looked at the clock in the corner. It was still early. She spotted the show manager across the room and went to have a few words with him, promising to return before the next performance.

It took only a few minutes in her room to pack some clothes and load her bags on her horse. She put her old Henry rifle in the scabbard. She knew how to use it if she had to. Five minutes later, Victoria was on the trail to Taylor.

# Chapter 4
## *Last Chance Saloon*

The *Last Chance Saloon* in Georgetown looked better than a whole lot of saloons I'd been in up to now. I wasn't sure whose last chance it was, but I was pretty sure it wasn't mine. Anyway, most things look good after two weeks on the trails, and saloons are up near the top of my list. I had nearly forty dollars in my pocket and a cold beer in front of me. Levi had gone off to see the sheriff, somebody named Ben Fiske, and I had some time to kill in this saloon.

I leaned back against the bar and studied the poker game going on at a table across the room. There were a few more tables, but those were empty. Only this one game was going on right now. The dealer looked pretty slick—he shuffled like he'd done it before. The cards flew off his fingers in all directions. There were two players at the table, and one of them was definitely doing better than the other one.

Across from the dealer sat a guy with a ruffled shirt and a sharp pair of eyes. There was a gold watch sticking out of his vest pocket. I studied the table for a while and decided that the dealer and the guy with the gold watch were working together. I had seen this kind of thing before. Everybody's so busy watching the dealer that nobody pays much attention to the gambler stacking up a pile of chips and never losing a big hand. The dealer would get his share later.

The other player at the table looked like a cowboy who was gettin' himself sheared. They would let him win a few small hands, then take the kid big. After half an hour, he was down to half his chips. I decided to help the kid and make a few bucks myself. Ma used to tell me sometimes I don't think things through. I guess this was one of those times.

I walked over to the table and laid down ten dollars. "Kin I join?" I drawled. Sometimes when they know you're from the hills, they think you're a pigeon. I laid on the Tennessee accent extra thick. The dealer shot a glance at the gambler with the gold watch and got a shrug. The dealer shoved some chips at me, and I took a seat.

I nodded at the kid, who paid me no mind. He was staring at the table with a red flush climbing up his neck. A quick glance told me everybody at the table was armed, including me, not that I expected it to come to a shooting. They would let me win a few small hands. I planned to take that money and skedaddle before they shook me down for the big bucks.

It was the kid that was messing up my plans. He was fool enough to stay in the game and mad enough to get hisself shot. The first hand came my way. I studied the cards and threw away two, holding on to a pair of jacks and an eight. The next two came. The kid folded, but the gambler took two cards also. I couldn't hear the whisper of cards coming off the bottom—I figured it was a clean deal.

I studied the new cards. He'd dealt me an eight and a three, giving me two pair. Had they set me up or not? I glanced around the table. The gambler raised me two dollars. I pushed in my two chips and called. When we turned the cards, my two pair had beaten a pair of sixes.

I raked in my chips and folded on the next hand. The kid was working on a fresh shot of whiskey and didn't seem to notice the slick bottom deal when it came his way. The other two made their bets, and the kids came away with four dollars. He brightened up and downed the rest of his whiskey, but I knew he was just being fattened up for the kill.

The next hand brought me a full house, nines over twos. I was pretty sure he'd slipped me one card off the bottom. The question was, were they going to let me win one more or take my money on this hand?

The kid raised a dollar, then folded when we both saw his dollar. The gambler raised me five and studied me while I thought it over. I decided they would fleece me later, and I called his five dollars. He showed a pair. I pulled in the money, but I figured the friendly game was over now. I was up nine dollars. It was time to go, but I stayed at the table because of the kid.

The other two both got cards off the bottom on the next deal. I was lookin' at a pair of threes, but that was just chance. The bottom deals had gone to the other two players. I knew they had set up the kid with a good hand, but the gambler would have a better one. I folded and waited. They went back and forth twice with their bets, then the kid cowboy went all in. When they turned the cards, he was showing a full house against four aces.

The kid flushed beet red and stared at the dealer. I eased my chair back and stood slowly, hands in full view. "I'm out," I announced. I looked across the table. "C'mon, kid, let's get some air," I drawled.

He shoved his chair back and stood. The dealer and the gambler stood too, staring at the kid. They exchanged glances. The dealer nodded at the gambler. I could see it coming, the kid would draw on the dealer, but the gambler would kill him when he did.

"You cheat!" the kid snarled at the dealer.

It was like it all happened at half speed. The kid clawed at his gun. The dealer's hand dropped to his side, but the gambler had already cleared leather. The boom from my own Colt was deafening. I barely knew I had drawn. I guess I had practiced enough with Levi to make it happen automatically. The gambler clutched at his chest and collapsed. The dealer whirled and stared at the dead man, gun half-drawn. The kid fumbled his gun, and it clattered onto the floor.

I took a half-step and shoved my gun into the dealer's ribs. "Drop it now or you'll join your pal," I advised. His gun slid back into his holster, and his hands went up in the air.

I stared across the table at the kid and nodded at the money on the table. "Leave me a couple dollars and take the rest," I told him. "I expect it's mostly your money anyway. He gave me a few dollars, like I said, then scooped the rest of the money into his hat and bolted out the door."

The kid had just scrambled through the batwing doors when they opened again, and a man with a tin star strolled into the saloon, followed by Levi Noone. The sheriff walked over to the table, looked at the dead man, then stared at me. "Tell me what happened here!" he barked.

I pointed at the dead man on the floor. "Him and Bottom Dealer here," I said, pointing at the dealer, "had themselves a crooked game going. Dealer was setting up the best hands for this guy." I nodded at the dead man. "They taken a kid cowboy for all his money. Kid went for his gun and they were gonna kill him. I shot this man first."

The sheriff wheeled around and looked at the bartender. "That the way it was?" he demanded.

The bartender nodded. "Pretty much like he said. Fair fight. They set up the kid."

The sheriff nodded slowly and turned back to stare at me. "You kin keep yore gun," he told me. "And I don't care if you stay around town for a while. I don't expect to see you playin' no more poker, though."

I nodded.

Now the sheriff turned and got into the dealer's face. "I done tole you about the crooked games," he growled. "Count yourself lucky he left you alive. I don't wanna see you again around here." He leaned in a little further. "Git!" he barked.

The dealer fled. Levi stepped over and patted me on the shoulder. "Glad to see you've made some friends," he drawled. He stepped over the dead gambler and moved toward the bar. "Whiskey is on me," he announced.

I stepped around the dead man slowly, staring at him as I moved. I'd never shot anybody except with a rifle and at a distance, and that was during the war. I took my time joining Levi at the bar. "I can use that whiskey," I admitted. I took one more look at the dead man and downed my free whiskey.

**\* \* \***

Victoria got in too late to look around the ranch, but her father insisted she ride along with him and her younger brother Rusty when they checked the cattle the next morning. It was good ranch land—they had always known that. Warm weather most of the year and enough rain to keep the grass growing, that was the key.

They paused by the stream that flowed across the property. Things looked peaceful enough, but she could tell her father was worried. No doubt it had to do with the Rolling R brand, just north and west of them. Carl Erskine was the man who owned the Rolling R. Victoria had heard they had nearly five thousand head of cattle. She knew that made them five times as big as their family ranch.

Her father sent Rusty off to repair some fence line. They both watched while he rode off to the west. Victoria knew this meant her father wanted to talk. He thought Rusty was too young to worry about things, and he didn't want her mother to worry either. That left Victoria to listen to him. It had always been that way, she reflected.

Her horse wandered to the stream for a drink. Her father, Matt, followed her to the stream. "Neighbors around these parts have always been peaceful," he said suddenly.

She knew there was more, so she just waited.

"Rossum family the ranch to the west, bordered

Rolling R, just like us," he said softly. "You remember them?"

Victoria nodded. Jeb Rossum, the oldest boy, had enjoyed pulling her pigtails at the little one-room schoolhouse they'd gone to. She grinned a little at the memory. Jeb was married and had himself a baby, the last she knew.

"Herb Rossum sold out, just about a month back," Matt growled. "Sold out to the Rolling R. Says he's moving the whole family to Austin. Dunno what he's gonna do over there. He's always been a rancher, just like me."

Victoria's eyes widened in surprise, and she swung her horse slightly to look at her father. "Did he tell you why?" she asked, even though she was pretty sure of the answer. Matt confirmed it moments later.

"Tired of fightin' with the Rolling R, that's what he told me. I seen him down at the general store in Taylor last week. Rolling R kept tryin' to push some of their cows onto his land, just like they do with mine. Said he thought mebbe a couple head of young'uns got poached." He lapsed into silence for a moment. "I tole Rusty and our hand Juan to keep an eye out. Dunno what we can do, though. They've taken to wearing pistols over there. I never have anything but my rifle, just usin' it for varmints. Rusty and Juan ain't armed."

Victoria looked across the pasture, watching the cattle graze. "You rounded up some cows and sent them on a drive to Kansas, didn't you?" she asked. "How did that turn out?"

Matt brightened a little. "Got a good price," he said. "Sent a hunnerd head north. Eighty-five of 'em made it and fetched almost thirty dollars a head in Abilene. Might do that again before long."

He leaned forward and rested his arms on the saddle horn. "Rossum done the same thing, he told me. Gettin' a good price for the cows helped him decide. Rolling R probably didn't pay everything the ranch was worth. Says he's got enough, though. I heard Erskine sent those cows and a thousand head of his up north." Matt pushed his hat back and shook his head. "Thing is, I'm a rancher. Don't wanna be nothin' else. Planned to leave this land to family."

Victoria reached over to place a hand on his wrist, and they sat side-by-side in silence for a while. Finally, Matt turned his horse for the house. "I expect your ma has a good breakfast by now," he announced. "Rusty's probly already halfway there."

The next two days went by in a hurry for her. She divided her time between helping her mother in the house and out in the garden, then helping her dad at the barn, shoeing horses, and helping break a colt to the saddle.

Victoria had expected to hear more from Margie, her mother, but she was strangely silent. Victoria wasn't sure what that meant, but her mom seemed resigned. Happy to have her daughter there, but resigned and tired.

By the time she was ready to return to Georgetown, Victoria had enjoyed the memories of how she had grown up, but she was also reminded of why she had left the ranch. This wasn't what she wanted for herself. When it was time to go, her mother walked her out to the corral to mount up.

Margie still hadn't spoken about their trouble with

the Rolling R, but Victoria could feel the sadness. Margie laid a hand on her arm at the gate.

"You were always the smart one," she said, "always the one that figured things out. You knew what you wanted and planned what to do. I know Matt has talked about the ranch and the troubles we're having. Write me when you have a chance. Tell me what you think about the Rolling R and our ranch. Tell me what you'd do. I just want the family together and happy."

Victoria leaned over to give her a hug before she rode out. By the time she'd reached Georgetown, she was no closer to having any answers. One road led to selling the ranch, which her father wouldn't do, and the other led to a range war they couldn't win.

* * *

Levi had ridden off on a bounty hunting job maybe a week and a half ago. He'd offered to bring me along as a partner, but I wasn't ready for that. I wasn't sure just yet what I wanted to do. Meanwhile, I got a job offer from a place I wasn't expecting.

The owner at the *Last Chance Saloon* decided he liked how I'd handled things at the crooked poker game. That took me by surprise. I'd left one of his best customers headed for Boot Hill, and the dealer wouldn't be bringing no more business to the saloon. Turned out, the owner, Bert, was glad to be rid of the both of them.

Bert had offered me five dollars a week to spell him at the bar, sweep the place up, and show the rowdies the fastest way out when they acted up. "Keep 'em throwed out," was what Bert told me.

He also let me sleep in the back room for free. He was smart enough not to give me free beer, though. Doesn't mean I didn't ask, mind you, but he was smart enough not to give it to me. Except for when I had to handle Buster. I got a free beer every time I threw Buster out. I didn't look forward to it, free beer or not.

Buster claimed he was half-man, half-bear. He was almost as big as a small bear, but he wasn't light on his feet. That was my ace in the hole. I could land three punches while he got himself set to swing at me. Sometimes, Buster just drank a few beers and left, all peaceful-like. Sometimes, though, like this afternoon, he drank whiskey and got mean when we cut him off.

He'd been at the bar for a while now and had slammed maybe three shots of whiskey. He waved for another, and Bert told him no. Buster let out a bellow of rage and slammed his fist on the bar.

"Nash," Bert yelled. He pointed at Buster.

"Nash again?" Buster roared. I came up behind him, and he put a new move on me. He came off his stool, wheeled around, and let loose a huge right hand all at once. He almost got me, too. I ducked just in time and lifted a right hook that started at my knees and finished on his chin.

Buster slumped back against the bar and slid down to the floor.

Bert looked over the bar and spotted Buster on the floor. "Good job, Nash!" he boomed. "Now, you know how Buster likes to sleep it off out back."

I sighed, grabbed Buster by the heels, and dragged him out the back door. I left him out in the alley behind the shops, sprawled out in the dust.

I stepped back inside just as Sheriff Fiske stepped

through the door. I'd cut a wide path around him ever since I'd shot that gambler last week.

"Somebody showed up at the sheriff's office and said Buster was causin' a ruckus down here," Fiske announced. "I come down here to deal with it. Where's Buster?"

Bert rubbed the bar with a rag and looked at me sideways. "Buster said he was tired, didn't he, Nash?"

I nodded my head up and down a few times. "That's right," I chimed in. "He's takin' himself a nap out back."

Sheriff Fiske stepped around me and opened the door to the back alley. He took a look outside, then closed the door and stepped back in. There was a tiny little grin on his face. "Well," he observed, "a man's got to get his sleep."

That's when I started to like Sheriff Fiske. He stopped at the door on the way out and looked back at me. "Nash," he said, "Levi Noone is back in town and thinks you might be interested in what we're gonna talk about. Come on down to the sheriff's office if you've a mind to."

I looked over at Bert. He just waved a hand in the air and slid a glass down the bar. "Take your beer with you," was all he said.

# Chapter 5
## *Victoria*

Sheriff Fiske headed for his office at a trot, and I couldn't keep up without spilling my free beer, so I took my time following. When he turned the corner, I stopped after a sign caught my eye in front of the Temperance Hall.

The sign said the show would be open tonight. Tickets were twenty-five cents. I felt around for the change in my pocket and decided I could spend it. There was a clown in the picture, juggling some rubber balls or something, but what caught my eye was the girl. She was singing, and she had the prettiest blue eyes and auburn-colored hair. I stopped to get me a better look at it.

"Purty, ain't she?" said a voice in my ear. I jumped and spilled some of the beer. I knew already it was Levi. I glared at him and slugged down the rest of the beer.

"I was looking at the juggler," I said.

Levi chortled and kept going to the sheriff's office. I've gotta admit, I don't know anybody who would have believed I was looking at the juggler. I trailed along behind Levi, set the beer glass down outside the sheriff's office, and followed Levi inside.

Ben Fiske leaned back in his chair, locked his hands behind his head, and waved us into chairs in front of his desk. He looked at Levi.

"You tell him about this yet?" Fiske was laughing, but I couldn't see how anything was funny right now.

"Nope." Levi swung around to look at me. "You remember you said you might want to help with the bounty hunting if it's good money and we don't have to traipse off to Arkansas or Indian Nation, or someplace like that, right?"

I nodded. "How much money?" was the first thing I asked. I believe in gettin' right down to what you want to know. It wouldn't take much to beat what I was making at the saloon, but I wasn't gonna give away my hand just yet.

"Fifty apiece. Hunnerd dollars total, an' it shouldn't take no more than four or five days." Levi stopped and checked to see if I looked interested. "You can't make no fifty dollars pullin' beers and mopping the floors down at the Last Chance."

"You wouldn't have to drag out Buster no more, either," Fiske assured me.

"Okay, I'm listening," I said. "Who would we be huntin' and what's he done?"

"Rustler," Levi said. "Could be dangerous, but I don't think so. He's jest pretty slippery and hard to catch, that's what Ben over here tells me. We've got to catch him and bring him back here."

I looked over at Fiske, and he seemed to be grinning underneath his mustache. I still couldn't see what was funny.

"How many head of cattle has he taken?" I asked. "Must be a bunch of 'em to get a hunnerd dollars put on his head."

"Twenty-five...sheep," Fiske said. He couldn't help himself anymore and busted out laughing.

"You boys'll have to chase down a big-time...sheep rustler." He lay across the desk and had himself a belly laugh.

I started to stand up. Levi threw up a hand to stop me. "Hold on, Nash, I'm serious about the money. This guy had been stealing some prize ewes from two different sheep ranchers out west of here. He takes 'em to the railroad and sells 'em to breeders out in Californy and places like that. That's what the ranchers think, anyway. They're desperate enough to pay good money 'cause they can't catch him. He disappears on 'em. Gone just like a ghost, that's what they say."

"Hold on, boys, I've got a poster." Fiske stopped laughing long enough to slide something across his desk. Levi reached for it, but I snatched it up first. I was staring at an old man with a long, scraggly beard.

I passed it over to Levi. "I don't think he's got any teeth," I muttered. "You sure this isn't a joke?"

Levi shook his head and passed the poster back to Fiske. "I'm serious, Nash. There's a couple of sheep farmers out there worried enough they've got a hunnerd dollars to give us once we deliver this guy...he looked over at the poster again...this guy named Ike to Sheriff Fiske here. You got somethin' better to do?"

I heaved a sigh and stood up. "Okay, I ain't got anything better to do. I better get fifty dollars for this." I moved toward the door. "When do you wanna leave?"

"Tomorrow morning," Levi shot back. "We meet

early at the diner for breakfast, then we go get this guy. Easy. You'll see."

The last thing I heard as I shut the door was Fiske laughing again. There wasn't even a last name on the poster. Just some sheep-stealer named Ike.

* * *

I wasn't fit to be seen by the likes of that girl I saw on the sign for the show. I hadn't had a shave or got into my Sunday-go-to-meeting clothes. Well, I didn't have any of those, but I hadn't even changed after mopping up at the bar this evening. I just came on over and paid my money. I was leavin' town in the morning, and I didn't know if the show would still be on when I got back. I coughed up my twenty-five cents and went in.

There were some sketches that were tolerably funny and one or two guys singing. I didn't care much about that. I was waiting for the girl on the sign. She came out after about a half hour and sang *Clementine*. My jaw dropped to my knees, I expect. She sang like an angel, and I hung on every word. Before it was over, she came back out and sang *Home on the Range*.

Then the show was over. Well, the clown came out to juggle and dropped two balls, but I'm not going to count that. The crowd started getting up, but I was just sitting there. I felt my scraggly beard, and I knew my hair was getting pretty long, too. I stared down at my britches, which had a couple of fresh beer spills from this afternoon.

I was in no shape to go try and meet that girl, but I was coming back, I was sure of that. I looked at the paper they gave me when I came in. Victoria Ridley, that was her name. I would come back when I could make a better impression. If the show was still in town after we chased down the sheep rustler, that is.

I filed out, and who should I see, walking down the street, but Levi. He stopped and grinned. "Gone to see the juggler, huh? How did he do?"

"Dropped a couple balls," I growled. I stared at the dog standing next to Levi. He was a hound of some kind with long floppy ears and sad eyes. While I watched, he sat down and started scratching his ear.

I pointed. "What's that?"

"That's Zeke," he told me. "Zeke's a tracking dog, ain't you, Zeke?"

Zeke rolled over with his belly in the air and waved all four paws at me. I rolled my eyes and kept going. I didn't want to talk about Zeke or the show.

"Tomorrow morning, at the diner. First thing!" Levi hollered.

I waved over my shoulder and kept going.

*  *  *

We met up at the diner just as soon as it was open. Levi and I ordered for ourselves, then Levi talked the cook into putting some of last night's beef stew in a bowl. He took it out and served it to Zeke, who was tied to a bench outside. I don't know why he needed to be tied. He wolfed down that stew, then flopped down and commenced to snoring right there.

After we had shoveled down our fill of the eggs and bacon, we drank coffee while Levi spread out a map on the table. I could see where Georgetown was drawn in, and it looked like Austin was down below Georgetown.

Levi pointed at two rivers meeting up in George-town, flowing in from the west. "Both of the sheep farmers are out here west of Georgetown and a little south," he said, pointing at the map. "Both of 'em pretty close to the South Fork of the San Gabriel River." He pointed again, and I nodded.

"The way I figure it," he continued, "what with those farmers saying he disappears like a ghost, is that he drives them sheep into the river. Neither of those north or south forks is very deep or fast. Maybe he's got him a sheepdog, maybe he don't, but he could drive those sheep along for a while, then move 'em out on the other side and cover over the tracks."

Now he circled a bigger area around the south fork of the river and pointed again. "The country gets a little hillier out here—that's why folks call it the Hill Country. There are some draws into canyons and maybe a cave or two. I think he might have a spot where he goes into one end of a draw and comes out the other. Goes down to Austin and sends 'em off to Californy, maybe."

"Okay, that makes sense," I said. "How are we gonna catch him?"

"That's where Zeke comes in," Levi told me proudly. "We'll bunk in at one of those sheep ranch places and then go see where the sheep were grazing when they was took. We'll do that at first light. We'll give ole' Zeke a whiff of what to follow. He can track the smell down to the river, then we'll cross and let him work along on the south side. If we can find where the sheep came out, we can catch this Ike guy."

I stared doubtfully out the window at Zeke. I could almost hear him snoring from here.

"You'll see," Levi insisted. "Zeke loves to track things. He'll show us where the sheep are."

We paid up and walked out. "Fifty dollars," I kept telling myself. "Fifty dollars."

Levi rousted Zeke out of his sweet dreams, and we mounted up and trotted out of town. Zeke loped along behind us. Well, I thought, at least he can run when he's of a mind to.

**\* \* \***

It took us two days to reach a place run by a guy who called himself Farmer Sid. Sid had several hundred sheep on the place and had prided himself on a few prize-winning ewes. He didn't have them anymore. According to Sid, they were likely on the way to California by now, and Sid was hopping mad. He had pooled his money with a neighbor to offer a hundred-dollar reward on a sheep rustler named Ike. At least that's who Sid and his neighbor were blaming it on.

We showed Sid the poster, and he swelled up and turned red, pointing at the poster. "That's him!" he bellowed. "I seen him skulkin' around here. You bring him to me an' I'll send him to a hot place where's he's bound to wind up anyway. I'll git him there a little sooner!"

We told him we'd have to take him to the sheriff when we caught him. Sid swore under his breath, stomped around for a while, then disappeared into the house. I stared at the house after the door slammed shut.

"Think he's gonna bring us any dinner?" I asked.

Levi shook his head. "I don't think he's got a Mrs.

Sid around here," he said. "We probly don't wanna see what it looks like inside that house, or eat what he cooks for supper. Maybe he'll bring us some breakfast."

We dug out a little venison and some biscuits for dinner, then bunked down in the barn. I staked Zeke outside after his snoring kept me awake. "You better be good at trailin' them sheep," I told him. Zeke rolled over for a scratch. I ignored him and went back into the barn to get some shuteye.

Early the next morning, Sid carried out some eggs and bacon for us, along with some terrible coffee. We sat down to eat at a table on the porch. Sid stared at Zeke. "Is he gonna trail the sheep?" he asked. "Looks like a bloodhound."

"Mostly bloodhound," Levi agreed. "Dunno what the rest of him is."

Sid got up to feed Zeke. He had sheepdogs around, of course, so Zeke got some sheepdog food. Sid came back with some fleece and handed it to me. "Give him a whiff of that when you set out," he advised. He pointed south. "My dogs trailed 'em down toward the river." He got up and disappeared inside. It was the last we saw of Sid.

I gave Zeke a good sniff of the fleece, then we moved out to the pasture where the sheep had been when the rustler struck. We moved south, letting Zeke cast back and forth. He didn't disappoint me. I saw him stop and sniffle for a while in the grass, then his tail came up, he howled twice, and set off toward the South Fork.

We got to the river in a hurry, but old Zeke came up short once he got to the water. He cast back and forth a few times, snuffled at the river a bit, then came running back to us, looking for directions, I expect.

Levi checked the depth and current in the river, then urged his horse in and picked his way across. The water wasn't above the horse's knees anywhere along the crossing. I followed with Cisco while Zeke splashed along beside us.

"We'll get to the south side and work along the bank," Levi called out over his shoulder. "Zeke should be able to pick up the scent where the sheep came out of the water. Saves us wandering back and forth trying to find tracks."

It took a while, but it worked out just like Levi expected. We worked our way along the south bank for a good hour. Ike had worked those sheep downstream quite a way, it looked like. Finally, Zeke's head went down for a good sniffle, he woofed twice, and took off.

We galloped along behind. Zeke was in full stride, head down, tail whipping back and forth. After fifteen minutes, he veered south, and Levi pointed at some low hills rising in front of us.

"Keep an eye peeled for a draw back into them hills," he shouted. "He might have been lookin' for a way to cut through and make for the railroad at Austin."

Zeke ran along without breaking stride, now headed for what looked like a narrow draw into a canyon. Levi looked over and grinned. I urged Cisco up beside him, then felt a sharp blow on my arm. The next moment, Zeke yelped in pain and turned, running back toward us.

I stared at Levi in total confusion. There had been no gunshot, I was sure of that. My arm was stinging, and Zeke was in full retreat. Levi shielded his eyes and looked toward the canyon, then cursed and ducked. A rock zinged past him and landed in the dust, skipping and rolling away.

We reined our horses back and out of range. Zeke took cover behind us. Another rock came close and we backed farther away.

"Who can throw a rock that far?" I demanded.

Levi chuckled and stared into the ravine. "Sling-shot," he explained.

"Slingshot?" I'd heard what he said, it just didn't make a lot of sense to me. "Who uses a slingshot?"

"Keeps from scarin' the sheep," Levi explained. "He might have a gun, but maybe not. He's just used to making a clean getaway and herding the sheep right down to the railroad." He frowned. "Didn't think he'd still have any sheep still around here, though. He took Sid's sheep a week ago."

"Neighbor," I guessed. "He might have taken some sheep from the other sheep farmer, the one down the trail from Sid. Might have got 'em last night."

I looked back along the hills, seeing where they sloped down to meet the ground, off to the east of us. I got an idea.

"I could ride around those hills and cut around to the back side of 'em, over there to the south," I suggested. "You give me maybe a half hour to get around to the other side of this ravine. I'll be waitin' for him over there. You send a few shots into the ravine after I get there and flush him out the other side. I'll bag him when he comes out."

I turned Cisco and galloped along the hills as they sloped down to level out. It was a gentle series of low hills, covered with wild grasses and dotted with scrubby live oaks now and then. When the hills leveled out, I cut across and moved west, looking for the other side of that ravine.

There! I heard the *baaah* of the sheep first. Four or five of them spilled out into the canyon, followed by a guy in a robe and scruffy beard. It had to be Ike. I raised my Henry rifle and fired a shot into the dirt in front of his feet. He skidded to a stop and lifted his hands in the air.

I kept the Henry trained on him as I rode up. I could see a forked stick in one hand with a leather strap hanging down. He had a rock in the other hand. "Drop the slingshot and the rock," I barked.

He stared at me, eyes glittering. I levered the Henry, and he dropped both.

"Turn around," I said, moving closer. I dismounted and went to check him over. He had a pair of britches under the robe with a small pistol in the waistband. I took that out and found a knife in a sheath strapped to his shin. I pulled that too.

Levi rode out of the canyon. Zeke trailed after him, looking wary.

I examined the gun I had pulled from his waistband. "Colt 1849 Pocket Revolver," I said, tossing it to Levi. I walked over and tucked the knife into my saddlebag. "Now," I said, looking around, "Ike, here, can help us gather up a few sheep."

He stayed right where he was, those eyes still glittering with hatred. Zeke walked over to sniff the prisoner. His head was right there at crotch level. He bared his teeth and growled. Ike went out to gather up the sheep. I was starting to like Zeke.

# Chapter 6
## *Meeting Goodnight*

Two days later, we turned Ike over to the sheriff in Georgetown and collected our reward. Sheriff Fiske just paid the money and locked up the prisoner without any questions. I took my money and left the office, but the sheriff asked Levi to stay behind. I took Zeke the hound back and left him at the house where Levi had found him—at a place outside of town. I paid the owner what we owed. Zeke wandered out to the front porch after I dropped him off and took a nap.

I had a feeling the sheriff was offering another bounty hunting job to Levi. I knew I would hear about it later and would have to decide if that's what I wanted to do. For now, I had almost a hundred dollars in my pockets and needed to think of something smart to do with it. I still had nothing to my name except Cisco, my saddle, and my gun.

I know where twenty-five cents of it would go. Actually, more like a dollar or two after I would get myself a haircut, bath, and a shave along with a new pair of britches. I had to see that show again. It was still in town at the Temperance Hall—I'd checked that first thing.

The diner was my next stop. Levi and I had been living on my cooking for more than a week now, and I could feel my belly rubbin' against my backbone. A good steak and some apple pie sounded like just what I needed. Then there was time after dinner to get myself presentable before the show. I might even spend fifty cents to get up in the front row. I'd heard you could pay a little extra money to do that.

The diner was pretty crowded, but I took my time over the steak. It was one of the best I'd had. Beef was easier to find down here in Texas, so that made sense. My apple pie came, and it was about halfway down the hatch when a shadow fell over my table.

A tall, dark-haired, good-lookin' guy was standing over my table. He scratched briefly at his short, trimmed beard and pointed at the chair across the table from me. "This place is really crowded," he said. "I'm headed out of town soon and wondered if I could sit at the table with you for some dinner."

I took another look at him. My ma would have said he was *well turned-out*, whatever that means. All gussied-up, I guess. He looked all barbered and dressed up like I wanted to look tonight. Maybe, I thought, I could get a couple tips from him.

I nodded. "Help yourself," I said. "I'm almost done anyway."

He sat down and held out his hand. "Charles Good-night," he said. "You can call me Charlie."

Now, where had I heard that name? I mean, I'm pretty new to Texas, and I haven't met a lot of folks, but I felt like I should know that name.

I swallered another piece of pie and shook his hand. "Nash Walker," I said. "I'm new to these parts. Should I have heard of you?"

He laughed, then stopped to tell the waiter he wanted some beef stew and a beer. "No reason you should," he said, turning back to me. "I don't live around here. I came to check on some cows I was thinking about buying."

That's when it hit me. "Cattle drives," I burst out. "You've done some cattle drives, 'ceptin' you don't go to Kansas. You been drivin' 'em up to Colorado. Denver and places like that."

He grinned. "That's right! My partner and I figured out a trail through New Mexico territory and up into Colorado. Good market for beef up there." His face turned a little sad. "My partner got killed by Comanches on the trail. Kinda dangerous. I'm still making drives, though. Just gotta keep your eyes open."

They brought him his beef stew, and Goodnight stopped talking while he tucked into his food. He waved a fork at me in between bites. "What about you, Nash? What do you do around here?"

I told him about the saloon work and catching the sheep rustler. He had a good laugh about that. "Truth is," I told him, "I've got about a hunnerd dollars burnin' a hole right through my pocket and I don't know what I want to do next. Maybe a little bounty hunting, but not for long. It's kinda like I'm a lawman, but not really." I stopped talking while he finished up his stew.

"You could buy some cows and take 'em to Colorado," he said. "You might need to buy some gear, some supplies and such. But you could take that hundred dollars and buy maybe twenty cows. Less if you need some gear for the trail. You could get to Colorado and still have thirteen or fourteen of 'em, with any luck. Sell them for four hundred dollars. That's a good start for whatever you wanna do next. A man could almost start a business or a ranch with that."

I stared at the table, thinking about that one. "Are you saying," I asked, "that I could maybe buy some cows, put 'em with your herd and join a drive to Colorado? I don't know the way up there and don't have an outfit."

Goodnight pulled a watch from his vest pocket to check the time, nodded, and stood. He left some money on the table for his food, then looked over at me. "Sure," he said, "I'm always looking for another good hand. My drives leave from Fort Belknap, out west of Ft. Worth. You could maybe find me around Fort Belknap, or ask the bartenders at the White Elephant Saloon in Ft. Worth. I'm usually around up there if I'm not on a drive."

He reached over and shook my hand again. "Good luck, Nash Walker." Then he was out the door. I dropped some money on the table and left. That was a lot to think about. Meanwhile, I had time for a haircut, shave, and a bath, not to mention some new clothes. I had decided on the front row tonight.

\* \* \*

Levi caught up with me on my way out of the barbershop. He stared at my fresh shave and took a good sniff at the lilac water the barber had splashed on me when he slicked down my hair.

A grin spread across his face. "Goin' back to see that

juggler, I can tell." He chortled. "Maybe that girl in the picture's gonna think you smell nice." He took another deep whiff, then dodged away when he saw the steam comin' out of my ears.

Levi waved a couple of posters he was carrying. "I come to talk about these horse thieves," he said. "Sheriff just told me about it. It's a good bounty hunting job. These boys are brothers, horse thieves, and they're wanted for killin' a man, too. Seventy-five dollars apiece." He pushed the posters at me.

I took the posters and sat down on a bench. Levi watched me. "Dead or alive," I mumbled to myself. I thought about the man I had killed during the poker game. "What if they don't come peaceful, Levi? What then?"

He sat down on the bench. "I won't shoot nobody unless it's to defend myself. I know you won't do that either." He waited while I looked at the posters again. "Sheriff thinks they're down in Austin. We can turn 'em into the Rangers down there. We'll just capture 'em and turn them in for a trial. Won't have to haul 'em all the way back here."

I stood and gave the posters back. "I'll think about it," I told him. "I'll let you know by morning."

I went down the street, stopped at the general store, and bought myself a new pair of pants, then stopped and looked at a building across the street when I came out of the store. It was a bank. I crossed the street and stood outside, feeling the money in my pocket and wondering if I should put the money in a bank. This was the first one I'd seen. I'd heard of 'em, but never saw one before.

I decided I felt safer with the money in my pocket

and headed down the street for the trading post. Wouldn't you know it, I almost ran into that girl from the poster on my way in. She dodged to the side to get out of my way. I grabbed my hat and twisted it up in my hands.

"Sorry, ma'am...I didn't see you comin'. I mean, I did, but sometimes I just get up a head of steam and I..."

She laughed and put a hand on my wrist. "Don't worry. I wasn't looking either, Mr...."

I was standing there passing my hat from one hand to the other when it dawned on me, I should introduce myself. I got my wits about me just in time.

"Nash, ma'am, Nash Walker."

She gave my hand a little squeeze and said her name was Victoria Ridley. "Just call me Victoria," she said. "I don't feel much like a ma'am."

I nodded and stopped passing the hat back and forth, but I couldn't think of what to say to her. She turned to leave.

"You sing like an angel," I blurted out.

She turned back, and a big smile spread across her face. "You've come to the show!" she said. "I don't guess I saw you there."

"I'll be back!" I burst out. I just managed to keep from fidgeting back and forth with my hat again. "I'll be in the front row tonight if I can get the ticket!"

That same huge smile was on her face. I ain't sure how I did it, but I think I'd said the right thing. She stepped closer and patted my arm again. "I'll look for you, Nash Walker," she murmured. Then she was gone.

Well, sir, I was standing there like I'd been pole-axed when I heard a chuckle from behind me in the trading post. I turned around to see Charles Goodnight, shaking his head and grinning at me.

"She's a pretty girl," he said. "I think you should take some flowers with you to that show. Stay around after and see if you can give her the flowers. She'll like that."

"Some flowers," I said stupidly, trying to remember where I'd seen some.

Goodnight chuckled again. "You could find some wildflowers growing around here. My wife always likes flowers. If you see a house with some nice flowers out front, maybe you could give the lady of the house two bits to pick some flowers and take them to the show."

He went on past me and turned back around. "If you get that front-row seat, make sure you've got those flowers where she can see them. In San Francisco, sometimes they throw flowers on the stage for the singers."

I stared after him. I wasn't too sure about throwing flowers on the stage. That might be a fool thing to do. Still, he might have a good idea about bringing flowers to the show. I went looking for a house with some flowers out front. I'd already got the bath, the shave, the haircut, and the new pants. What did I have to lose?

\* \* \*

The lady at the house where I picked the flowers must have decided she was my mother or something. She looked pretty confused when I knocked and asked about the flowers, so I just sucked it up and explained.

Well, then she came out of the house to help. I started for the first bunch of flowers I saw in the garden out front, but she steered me away and told me those weren't good enough. She pointed at some yellow roses. That was kind of a relief, really, on account I didn't know what any of the other flowers were called. I knew about roses.

She helped me pick the roses, pulled off the thorns, and wrapped them in a wet towel for me. She wouldn't take my money and sent me off with a piece of chocolate cake. You'd have thought I was giving them flowers to her.

I got my ticket for the front row, but it cost me extra. Some guy duded up in a suit and wearing a pair of spectacles told me it would cost me seventy-five cents. I'm pretty sure I saw the extra two bits go into his pocket, but I got my seat.

Anyway, I was ready for the show to start, right out in the middle of the front row. I was close enough to throw a rose at the stage, but I wasn't sure I was gonna do that. What if Goodnight was just funnin' me? He might have laughed all the way back to his hotel room.

The show went by in a hurry. Victoria Ridley came out and sang the first number, *Clementine*, and I clapped and cheered my head off. I'm pretty sure she saw me down here. When she finished *Home on the Range*, everybody was cheering, and she walked closer to the front of the stage. I grabbed a rose and heaved it up there.

Victoria stopped, picked up that rose, and waved it in the air. Then, I'm pretty sure she winked at me. The light wasn't real good, so I couldn't be sure, but I think she winked at me. The show ended, and I hung around, holding on to those flowers and waiting to see if I could catch her coming out.

\* \* \*

Victoria had found news from home in the letter waiting for her at the post office this morning, and it hadn't been good news. Their only hired hand had quit after being threatened by Rolling R hands. Victoria's mother was asking if she knew anyone to come work for them, somebody who could stand up to the Rolling R thugs.

Victoria worked with the vaudeville show people. How would she know anybody like her mother was describing, somebody who could stand up to gunhands? Those were the things on her mind when she'd come out of the trading post this morning. The young man who'd told her she sung like an angel had lifted her spirits more than he could know.

Now, she could see him out in the front row, just where he'd said he would be. That put a smile on her face as she belted out the finish to *Home on the Range*. Then he threw a flower onto the stage! She picked it up and winked, then hurried backstage to change. The girls who worked the show with her always said she should make the guys work harder—pretend like you're not interested when they come around after the show, they said. Victoria didn't really think that sounded like a good idea.

She was a ranch girl who had worked hard for anything that had come her way. He'd had a whole lapful of flowers out there, and he had thrown one to her. She figured there was only one way to find out if the rest of the flowers were for her.

Victoria was the first one of the actors to leave after the show. She spotted the guy standing over there, still holding the handful of yellow roses. He'd said his name at the trading post. She headed directly for him, searching her brain for that name, then it came to her.

"Nash!" she called. "Are those roses for me?"

* * *

I had been practicing in my head what I wanted to say when Victoria came out after the show. Seeing as how I'd already told her she sings like an angel, I didn't seem to have any other ideas running around in my head.

"They are for you." I straightened up and handed her the flowers. A couple other guys had been hanging around, and they started over toward us now. They reminded me of that hound Zeke, just casting back and forth and trying to get a scent.

I was saved from having to run those boys off when Victoria smelled the flowers, linked her arm through mine, and announced she was going to get some dinner. "Do you like the diner, Nash?" she asked. I expect I would have settled for some scraps behind the diner if she had come with me.

As it was, we just walked off, arm-in-arm, pretty as you please. I decided right then and there that Charles Goodnight knew exactly what he was talking about. I might need to look him up for more advice someday.

We settled down in the diner and both ordered some beef stew, then she leaned across the table and started asking me about myself. I got downright chatty, which ain't nothing like me, but it was like my throat was greased. I told her about the war and the moonshining and how I wasn't sure what to do with myself here in Texas. I finished up with the bounty hunting.

She had a serious look on her face. "These two men in Austin, they're dangerous, aren't they?" she asked. "Are you going to go?"

I fidgeted around a little, then nodded my head. "I expect I will," I told her. "I can take care of myself. Maybe I can use the money to get myself a little stake from that for something better."

"Like what?" She was still leaning in, watching my face while I talked. I decided I liked that.

I told her about Charles Goodnight and the cattle drives to Denver. Her face lit up a little, and she nodded.

When I finally ran down and stopped blabbering, she told me about the family ranch back home and how she didn't want to be a rancher. She told me about the Rolling R ranch and how she worried about her family. I got a little hot under the collar, thinking about that outfit crowding her family out.

"If your family needs some help," I told her. "You just let me know and I'll surely come a-foggin' it."

She laughed and patted my arm. "I'll let you know," she said. Then she surprised me. "I'm going to Austin, too," she announced. "I just found out today. We'll finish up here in Georgetown in a few more days, then we're going to do the same show at the Millett Opera House in Austin. You come and see me there."

I told her I would be there every night I could, and she laughed again. I liked that sound. I could get used to hearing that laugh. I don't rightly remember a lot else that we talked about. What I remember is walking her back to her boarding house with her arm through mine again.

# Chapter 7
## *Holdup in Progress*

Levi found me in a café down the street from the diner where we'd been stopping in to eat for the last several days. I was at this new place on purpose—I didn't want Levi to find me and spoil my good mood. I was in such a good mood, I wasn't even sure Levi could spoil it, but I didn't want to find out.

I was on my second cup of coffee and thinking about going to see Victoria down in Austin when Levi came through the door, shaking the rain off his hat and coming my way when he saw me in the corner.

"Coffee," he said to the girl behind the counter. He pulled out a chair and parked himself across the table, eyeing my breakfast. He swiveled himself to look at me. "Mornin'!" he barked.

"Mmmphh," I said, biting off a piece of muffin and waiting for him to ask about last night. Then it dawned on me he had no idea I had met Victoria. He had nothing to razz me about. I brightened up considerably and waited to see what he would say about the brothers and the bounty hunting. I could use the money, but I didn't want to get my fool head shot off.

He took his time, slurping on his hot coffee and ordering enough food to feed about two men his size. Finally, he got around to it.

"You been thinkin' about chasing down them boys in Austin? Lotsa money for us."

I pushed some eggs around my plate and forced myself to think about it some more. I hadn't wanted to spoil my good mood so early, so I hadn't given it much thinking up to now.

"You said you didn't wanna shoot anybody exceptin' in self-defense," I reminded him. "Just how likely do you think it is you and me will have to defend ourselves against these brothers? What're their names? How salty are they?"

"Barker," Levi said through a mouthful. "Ned and Sal Barker." He chewed thoughtfully and took another slurp of the hot coffee. "Dunno how likely they are to shoot unless we back 'em into a corner. I expect they've done some shootin' in their time."

He left that thought just hanging in the air and went back to shoveling food. I made a little moaning noise and leaned back in my chair, just waiting to hear the worst. At least the chicken rustler only used a sling-shot. Okay, I know they were sheep rustlers, but I was still mad at Levi about that job.

"The thing is, they robbed a brand-new bank down in Galveston. *The American National Bank of Texas*, that was the name of it." He frowned while he thought that one over. "Is it just in Texas or is it really national, like the whole United States?"

I didn't like where this one was going. I ignored his question. "They're gonna rob a bank in Austin?" I asked.

"Seems likely," he agreed. "The same folks have got them a brand-new bank in Austin, too. Same name as the other one." He looked puzzled again. "Don't know how come two of 'em have the same name. Sounds like they're really two different banks. Anyway, the sheriff and them Texas Rangers think they might have it in mind to rob another one. Those boys got almost five hunnerd dollars the first time."

"Why in Austin?" I asked. "There are other banks. Georgetown even had a bank."

Levi finished eating and looked across the table. "Sheriff can answer that one if you want to come to his office," he offered. "Plus, there's a Ranger down there. A real Texas Ranger. He offered to dep-u-tize us if we wanna go after these boys. We'd git badges and everything."

I sighed, threw some money on the table, and stood up. "That just sounds like a badge on my chest somebody can use for target practice," I growled. "Okay, I'll go down there with you. I haven't figured out why just yet." I trailed out the door after him.

I gotta admit, though, I never thought a moonshiner from Tennessee would ever be wearing a badge down here in Texas. I wondered if Ma would be proud. I decided she would be. Then I wondered if Victoria would like it.

Ben Fiske was in his office, chatting with a short, blonde-headed guy who looked as stout as a beer barrel when he stood up. "Fred Murphy," the Ranger said, sticking out a hand. "You can call me Murph. Ever'-body else does. Sit, please." He pointed at a couple of chairs.

Murph passed two posters across the desk to me. I held them out to Levi, who shook his head. "Already seen 'em," he murmured. I stared at the faces until I was sure I would know them if I saw 'em, then folded up the posters and put them in my pocket. Dark hair, heavy eyebrows. Mean eyes. I would remember.

"Levi's told you they robbed a bank in Galveston?" Murph asked. I nodded.

"Guvnor don't much like that," Murph growled. "He wants 'em caught, but most of our boys are tied up down at the border or up in Palo Duro Canyon. I can deputize you boys, give you badges and an extra ten dollars for your troubles. Guvnor don't want no Jesse James kinda stuff down here in Texas."

I glanced over at Levi. "Why do you think they might be in Austin?" I asked.

Fiske opened a drawer, dug around in some papers for a minute, then tossed one piece of paper across the desk to me. "Found this in the boardinghouse where they holed up after they robbed the bank in Galveston," he explained. "They had to clear out of town in a big hurry, and this got left behind."

I picked up the paper and moved to hold it in the light from the window. "Street map," I said, trying to read the street names. There were several names, but it wasn't anyplace I had ever been. One street name was circled. "Congress," I said, feelin' kinda pleased with myself. Those three years of school might be worth it after all.

I looked around. "Where is this?" I asked. "What town is it?" Then I knew, just as soon as I asked. "Austin." They all nodded. I looked back at the map. "What's on Congress Street?"

"Lots of things," Murph answered. "They're maybe gonna build a new Capitol building there. Other government buildings an' such are going in. A saloon or two. A hotel and some shops. What we think the Barker boys are interested in is the new bank. Called *First American National Bank of Texas*. Just like the one they robbed in Galveston."

"Why would they rob this second one?" I asked. "Doesn't seem real smart. People will be watching for another robbery there."

"Nobody ever accused 'em of bein' smart," Murph snorted. "Whatever they're after, Congress Avenue in Austin seems like the place to look, what with the way they circled that on the paper. We're guessing it's the bank." He glanced back and forth at us. "Levi says you know how to use a six-shooter."

"Am I gonna need it?" I asked.

"Maybe." Murph nodded a couple times. "They're downright mean if they're likkered up. Sloppy, though, after some whiskey. They drink to get up some courage, that's what they say. But you'll be lookin' for them and they won't even know about you. That's your advantage. Just bring 'em in and get your money."

I stared at the desktop and drummed my fingers for a while. I thought about what I could do with that money. Maybe it wasn't enough money to buy cows and join Goodnight, but I could get closer to doing that. Then I thought about being in Austin while Victoria was down there. I had nothin' else I could do to earn my keep hereabouts except swab the floors and pour beer at the saloon.

When I looked up, I realized all of them were staring at me. I nodded my head and put the map in my pocket, along with the posters. Murph pushed two badges and twenty dollars across the table. "Welcome," he barked. "You boys are temporary Rangers."

We stopped on the porch outside the office, and I pinned the badge to my shirt. Might as well get official right away, I thought.

Levi stopped beside me, pulled his pistol from the holster, and handed it over. "Lookee what I've got here," he said proudly.

I took the gun, looked it over, spun the cylinder and sighted down the barrel. I whistled. "It's that new Colt you were talkin' about, ain't it?" I spun the cylinder again and tested the weight of it in my hand. It felt good.

"They've got 'em down at the general store, just come in last week," Levi said. "They cost twenny dollars, but when I told 'em I'm a dep-u-tee Texas Ranger, he sold it to me for seventeen. He'd do the same for you."

I stared at the Colt, and Levi nodded his head toward a store down the street. "They got themselves a firin' range behind the store," he said. "You can fire it off, and I'll show you how to reload it. Easy as pie. You won't believe it."

We tried it out on the range. It felt light in my hands, and didn't pull or kick back at me much, either. When Levi reloaded, I just stared. Quick as a wink, that cylinder was full. I took one of the cartridges and turned it in my fingers.

"The hard work is all done," I mumbled, thinking about how long it took to pour the powder and load the cap and ball.

"You got seventeen dollars, right?" Levi asked, putting the gun back in the holster. "Might just save yore hide someday."

Fifteen minutes later, I forked over the money for a brand-new Colt and a couple boxes of cartridges. I was feelin' a little better about facing up to the Barker boys if we had to do that.

"You need the gun belt," Levi advised me. "It's got places to hold the cartridges." He pointed at his own. I sighed and passed some more money across the counter.

The general store owner leaned on the counter while I forked over my money. He grinned at both of us. "I expect I'll see you boys back here afore long," he said, tucking his money into a cigar box. "Gonna have them new Winchester 73 rifles."

Levi's eyes lit up. "I've heard somethin' about those guns. "Tell me more about 'em."

"Lever action!" the shopkeeper boomed. "No more of them bolt-action rifles and whatnot. Lever and fire, just like that. It'll hold twelve, maybe fifteen cartridges. Way more shots without reloading. And here's the best part." He leaned over the counter. "It'll take the same ammo as them Colt revolvers."

Levi's mouth was hangin' open and his eyes were shining. "When are you gonna get some in? What are they going to cost?"

The shopkeeper shrugged and shook his head. "I've got some ordered. Dunno when they're gonna get here.

Everybody I know who owns a store wants to get their hands on some. I ain't heard the price, but maybe twice what them Colts cost. I'll make you boys a deal, though, when I get some. I always make a deal for the Rangers."

Levi was babbling about the Winchester 73 halfway down the road to Austin. Wouldn't shut up for nothin'. Me, I was just wondering how much of my bounty money I was going to wind up spending on guns.

\* \* \*

I was expecting to be a little more impressed when we rode into Austin, it bein' a state capital an' all. We found our way to Congress Avenue, and there was a little more going on there than what I saw when we first rode in. Folks were comin' in and out of shops and stores and such, which made it pretty busy. I stopped and looked at a limestone building down the street. State Capitol building, that's what they told me. They had plans to build a new one to replace this one.

They'd had some rain here lately, so the ladies were having to hold up their skirts to cross the street. Gravel and mud, that's all they had for streets. I thought maybe there would be some bricks, but nope, just gravel and mud. They had boardwalks in front of most of the shops, so I guess that helped the ladies keep their dresses from getting muddy.

Levi and me slogged across the street. Our boots were as muddy as they could get already. As we stepped up to the boardwalk, Levi tapped my shoulder and pointed. *American National Bank of Texas* was what the sign said. And sure enough, it was new.

Levi shook his head. "Sign still confuses me," he confessed. "How can it be national if it's just in Texas?"

I didn't have any help for him there. I studied the building. It was brick instead of wood. A big hitching rail stood out front. A pair of horses was hitched to the rail, and a buggy with a driver was waiting just down the street. It sat at the end of the block, with a cross street on one side and a narrow alley down the other side. I knew there must be an alley out back.

"We ain't really got a plan for catching these Barker boys," I pointed out to Levi. "We gonna sit outside the bank and wait to catch 'em coming out when they rob it?" I scratched my head. "Maybe hang out in that saloon two buildings over and see if we can catch 'em gettin' likkered up before they try?"

"Hmmm." Levi took off his hat and gave his own head a scratch. "I ain't never gone after bank robbers before. Train robbers, I jest ride the train and wait. Stagecoach robbers, I hide at a likely spot in the trail and wait for 'em."

He put his hat back on his head and swung around to look at the saloon I had pointed out. "Let's you and me go in there and figger it out," he said.

Two beers apiece later, we weren't any closer to anything I'd call a plan. Levi liked the idea of catching them in the saloon, but there were a lot of saloons in town. How were we gonna know which one they might go to?

Levi shook his head and told me they were bound to come to the one closest to the bank. I thought since we had badges, we should just go over to the bank, talk to the president, and warn him about a robbery. Maybe, I said, he would have an idea we could use.

We stopped to get some supper and then got rooms at a boardinghouse, then went back to arguing about how to do this. Finally, I came up with an idea we could both agree to. Well, we almost agreed.

Next day, I would go to the bank, show my badge, and talk to the manager. Levi would go back to the saloon and pretend to get some kind of job, tending bar or sweeping up. We figured the badge would help him get some cooperation with the owner at the saloon. He would keep an eye out for the Barkers there.

We went back to that saloon and drank a couple more beers to celebrate. Lucky for us, the Barker boys didn't show up that night.

Neither one of us was up with the chickens that next morning, but the bank opened sooner than the saloon, I was sure of that. I walked across to the diner for some breakfast, then went back to my room.

I just couldn't decide if I should wear my most respectable clothes to impress the bank president, meaning the ones I had bought for Victoria's show the other night, or just wear my trail clothes. If I wore the trail clothes, my new Colt would be in the holster. I decided to wear the trail clothes and the Colt. The badge should be enough to get the banker's attention and help, even if I didn't have fancy clothes.

The bank had been open about an hour when I crossed the street and opened the door. I had been practicing what I would say to the owner, or manager, or whoever was there. I had the posters in my pocket. I had to ask first thing if the Barkers had already been in the bank and looked things over.

I stepped inside, and the door had swung shut behind me before my brain could tell me what my eyes were looking at. There were two guys with bandanas over their mouths. One was holding a gun to a man's back, pushing him over to a vault that was standing open. He had his back to me.

The second guy was about half-turned away from me. He had a canvas bag open, holding it with two hands, but he also had a gun in one hand. A woman was dropping money into the bag. My hand dropped toward my Colt as soon as I saw him, and the woman's eyes got big. She dropped the money on the floor.

The robber swore at her and moved like he was gonna bend over and get the money, then he looked back and saw me. He dropped the bag and swung his gun toward me, but mine was already out and level. The first shot from my Colt drove him back against a money cage. The second one knocked him over backward.

He struggled to get up, trying to get his gun level. I fired a third shot between his eyes, and he was done.

I swung to look at the vault just in time. The second robber came out and snapped a shot off at me. I felt the bullet burning across my neck. I fired back too soon. It went over his head, and he dove back into the vault.

His hand appeared around the corner of the vault to take a blind shot at me. I took aim and fired. He swore, dropped the gun, and the hand disappeared. I thought I might have creased his hand. Sure enough, a bloody hand shot out to retrieve the gun from the floor before I could fire again. He was out of sight, in the vault, and he still had a gun.

I crouched behind a desk to get a little cover. Just out of habit, I counted my shots. I shot fired five times. It was awful quiet in there. I let loose a short, nervous chuckle when I remembered I had the new Colt and could reload right away. I didn't need to worry so much about counting shots. That's when it hit me. What if he'd counted, too? What if he thought I just had one more shot in the gun before I was out of action and reloading?

# Chapter 8
## *Town Hero*

Somebody had crawled across the floor to stop the teller from screaming. She still stared across the floor at me, eyes as big as saucers. I could smell the gunpowder and sweat and fear in the room. It was quiet now that the teller had stopped screaming—too quiet to suit me.

I reached down to my new gun belt and pulled a cartridge. I flipped the cylinder open, just hoping the other robber didn't choose right now to come flyin' out of that vault. I risked a glance over there. Nothing was happening. Then I started feeding cartridges.

It felt like a couple of minutes, but I don't guess it took more than a few seconds to reload the Colt. I snapped the cylinder shut and looked over at the vault again. Still nothing moving. I didn't want to shoot blindly into the vault. I didn't know how many folks were in there, and I might catch an employee with the ricochet. I knew the robber had pushed at least one guy ahead of him into that vault. There could be more.

Aiming at the wall across the room, I squeezed off one shot and waited. If he thought my gun was empty, now was the time to make his move. The echo boomed through a quiet room.

Sure enough, he let out a fearsome yell and came screaming out of that vault. He snapped off a shot, but he didn't have a good look at me before he shot. I was on one knee, Colt steadied between my two hands, crouched next to a desk. He saw me right then and screeched to a halt, but not before I shot him right through the heart. He dropped like a stone. The bag he was carrying fell to the ground beside him. His gun clattered loudly on the floor.

Somebody came running out of the vault and yanked open a desk drawer. I was afraid he was looking for a pistol. I didn't need that. I jumped to my feet and pointed at the badge on my shirt pocket.

"Deputy Ranger!" I hollered. "Everybody, stand still! Both robbers are down!" I stepped around the desk and picked up the two pistols lying on the floor. I wanted to be holding the only gun left in this room.

The guy across the room left off searching in his desk drawer and stepped across the room, staring at my gun and my badge, in that order. I holstered the Colt.

"Abe Cross," he said. "I'm the owner of this bank, and I'm mighty glad to see you!"

He stared at the two dead men. "How did you know about these robbers? I mean, how did you know they'd be here?"

"I didn't," I confessed. "We had a hunch they were coming here, and well, the timing of this thing was just pure luck."

Abe Cross sent somebody off to get the undertaker and the sheriff, hung a *Closed* sign in the door, and sent everybody home, including that screaming teller. I wasn't sorry to see her go. Between the gunshots in a small room and all the screaming from her, my ears were gonna be ringing for a while.

Levi came galloping into the room about a minute after things settled down. "I saw the bodies they hauled off!" he barked. "That was both of 'em. Both of the Barker boys!" He settled down enough to look me over. "You good?" he asked. "Must have done some mighty fancy shootin' with that new gun."

When I told him I was okay, he charged back out the door. "Gonna find the sheriff!" he hollered over his shoulder. "And the Rangers! Gotta make sure they get down to the undertaker's and get a good look at those mugs before he plants those boys." Then he was gone. I had a feeling we would have the reward money by dinnertime.

I accepted a cup of coffee from Abe Cross and sipped it slowly. I looked down at the Colt Single Action Army revolver in my holster. Buying that might have saved my life. I knew I'd be buying the Winchester 73 rifle when it came out, too. I wanted every advantage I could get from now on.

The sheriff came in, and I went through what had happened. His eyebrows went up when I told him it was the same brothers who had held up the bank in Galveston. He wrote down my name, looked at my badge twice, and listened to the bank manager tell the same story I did. Then he went off to see the undertaker.

Abe Cross came over and put a hand on my shoulder. "It's not quite noon," he said, "but I'll buy the first beer they pour over at the saloon. Least I can do. We had a lot of money in that vault." He pointed toward the saloon I'd been at with Levi last night.

I got up and went out the door with him. "I'll let you do that," I told him. "Might even let you buy me two."

$$* * *$$

By the time we got to the saloon, Abe Cross had fished out his wallet and ordered up a pitcher of beer. He drank a couple glasses with me, then said he had to get back to the bank and put things back where they belonged. I guess that meant getting the money back in the vault.

Before he left, Abe said he was going to have the café down the street send me a steak. He patted me on the back a couple times. "You don't have to get up or anything," he said. "They'll bring it to you." He hurried out the door.

I was looking at most of a pitcher of beer left on the table and wondering how Levi hadn't gotten wind of this and parked himself to drain that pitcher. I guess I should have known a pitcher of beer will attract folks to the table, because somebody else showed up.

"Nash, right? Nash Walker?"

I looked up at somebody who looked a little familiar, but I couldn't tell you where I'd seen him. He pointed at the chair Abe had just left, and I nodded. I couldn't finish that pitcher all by myself, anyway.

"First Tennessee Infantry, right? We was in the thick of things at Shiloh?"

I stared across the table, trying to remember that face. He sure enough had an accent like mine. I nodded slowly. "Yeah, during Shiloh, I was with the First Infantry. Transferred a little while after."

"Yeah, went off to be horse soldier, din't ya?" He extended a hand across the table. "Shadrach Taylor. Sam Freeman's unit. Folks called me Shade."

I still didn't remember him, but I'd wiped out a lot of memories I had after that war. I shook his hand and pushed the pitcher his way, wondering what he was doing here. My gut told me he wanted something.

He took a pull at the beer and smacked his lips. "Never too early for some suds, that's what my pa always said." He refilled and stared at me, head cocked to one side. "Word is you done some fancy shootin' over at the bank this mornin'."

It was my turn to stare. How could he know about that already?

He shrugged and gave his beer some more attention. "Word gets around," he mumbled. He leaned around the table and looked at my pistol. "Got one o' them new Colts, I see," he observed. "Sounds like you knew what to do with it."

I watched him, still wondering what he wanted from me. "Nash Walker," I said finally. "I don't remember you from Shiloh, but there's lots I don't remember from them three days."

He nodded. "I run into the bank president out there and asked him who done the expert shootin' during the robbery. He tole me, an' that's when I remembered you from the war. I come to offer you a job. We can use a man who can take care of hisself."

"I ain't a gun hand," I flared. "Got no interest in bein' one. I took a temporary job and did what I was hired to do. That's it. Don't want no more jobs shooting and gettin' shot at."

He threw a hand up in the air. "Not a gun hand. We just need some cowboyin' done. Boss is partial to boys who was in the war, that's all. Got us a big ranch out east of here. Five thousand head of cattle, maybe more. Always lookin' for more help."

That sounded better, but it still didn't seem quite right. "Ain't done any cowboyin'," I said. "We had a couple cows, off and on, but they just stayed in the pasture and ate grass until we needed the beef. No ropin', no driving a herd, nothing like that." Part of me still wondering how he could remember me. That battle was a long time ago.

"Hold on," he said. "I'm still thirsty."

He stood and went for another pitcher. He had just one gun on him, but there was a second holster on that belt. It was empty right now. I wondered where the other gun was. Did he leave it in the saddlebag when he came to town?

Shadrach Taylor came back, sat down, and talked about the ranch for a while, telling me there would be some fence repair, some shootin' varmints—coyotes and such. "That's where it would come in handy, you knowin' how to shoot. Ropin', driving herds, branding— I kin teach you that myself. Hard to find good hands. We'd be glad to have you."

I didn't really know what I wanted to do next, and I told him so. We left it like that. I didn't have enough money to buy cows and join Goodnight on a drive if I got the Winchester 73, but maybe I could save a little dough and learn a few things this way.

Taylor pushed back from the table and stood.

"You kin just let me know," he said. "Offer's good. I got to get back, but you can ask anybody how to git to the Taylor spread. Jest show up an' ask for Shade Taylor."

I watched him leave, wondering what else this day would bring. It wasn't even one o'clock yet. I didn't have to wait long to find out.

* * *

Abe Cross was as good as his word. A steak showed up from the café and I didn't waste no time putting that steak where it belonged. I had just finished eating and started wondering about taking the dishes back to the café when Levi showed up, along with a guy with a badge. It was another Ranger.

Levi took a seat and pushed some money across the table at me. It was the reward for the Barker boys. I glanced at it, put it in my pocket, and looked at the guy with the badge, who'd helped himself to the seat Shade Taylor had just left.

I reached up to take the badge off my shirt and put it on the table. I'd noticed Levi didn't have his on anymore. The Ranger left the badge on the table where it was. "You can keep wearin' that if you'd like to," he said.

Levi pointed at the lawman. "This here is Cap'n Leander McNelly," he said. "I said I knew where to find you. You boys can talk." Levi wandered over to the bar. McNelly watched me across the table.

"Those Barker boys were said to be pretty handy with a gun," he said suddenly. "I talked to Abe Cross and the sheriff, but you tell me what happened in the bank this mornin'." He gave me a quick glance. "Looks like you come out of it without a scratch."

I walked him through the morning at the bank, surprised when I remembered a couple details I hadn't thought about before. McNelly stopped me when I talked about the first robber swinging his gun around on me.

"Was your gun out?" he asked.

I thought about it and shook my head. "Not yet. I was drawin' mine as he came around." McNelly's eyes dropped to my gun belt.

"He didn't get off a shot," he murmured. He waved his hand to go on. "The witnesses at the bank said the same thing you're sayin'," he told me. "Tell me the rest."

He grinned just a little when I told him about the new Colt and the six shots and my fast reload. I finished the story and waited.

McNelly leaned forward and pointed at the badge on the table. "I told you to keep that if you wanna," he said. "You think fast and you were plenty fast with that gun. And you hit what you aimed at. Kept a clear head, too." He stopped and squinted at me. "Just one shot at that second robber, right?"

I nodded. "I was set and ready for him."

McNelly nodded. "I can use another man if you're interested. I'll likely be formin' up a special unit. Maybe border patrol and problems with Mexican bandits and things like that. If we get more bank robberies, maybe we'll deal with some of those, too." He stopped and looked over at Levi, who had just come back to the table. "I know your partner over here just wants to do the bounty huntin', but he thought maybe you don't want that. I'm offering the badge, permanent if you're inclined."

That one took me back for just a smidge. I could see myself doing it, and I kinda liked McNelly. He seemed like a straight shooter. I couldn't see myself doing it right now, though. I had killed two men this morning. I didn't feel bad about it—they would have killed me. Still, it took some getting used to. How many mornings would be like this one?

I told McNelly I would give it some thought for down the road, but for right now, I was likely gonna do some ranch work and cowboyin'.

He nodded and held out his hand. "You change your mind, Walker, I want to know about it. I ain't likely to be around here in Austin, but Murph might be around, or you can just ask at the office in Austin. I'll remember you."

He put on his hat and left. I stared over at Levi. "That's two job offers just today," I said. I told him about Shadrach Taylor and the ranch offer. Levi stared at the ceiling. "I've heard of the Taylor outfit, I think," he mused. "Big outfit."

With that, Levi headed for the door. He stopped and turned around partway there. "By the way, pard," he said. "I saw a big sign over near the new opera house. There's a show in town. That...uh...juggler you like to watch. Looks like they got them a show starting tonight." Then he grinned and disappeared through the batwing doors. I could hear him laughing outside the saloon.

\* \* \*

Victoria stood outside the post office and eagerly tore open the letter from her mother. Victoria had only just today arrived in Austin and the letter was a pleasant surprise. She could only hope the news inside was good. If her family needed her, she would have to leave the show and go home to help in any way she could.

She relaxed as she read the first few paragraphs. There had been no recent trouble with the Rolling R, and her mother was hopeful things would settle down. They had hired a new hand—his name was Alec.

Her father said Alec had been *up the creek and around the bend in his time*—Victoria smiled at that one. It sounded like Alec was a no-nonsense old coot, which she knew her father would appreciate. He was like that himself.

The last paragraph took her by surprise. Austin was as close to home as any performance Victoria would do, and her mom was determined to come see her. Her father and brother had to stay and watch over the ranch, but Alec had volunteered to accompany her mother to Austin. They would be here for her first performance. That was today!

Victoria whirled and ran back inside to look at the clock in the post office. She had only about two hours to get ready for the show. There was no way to meet her mother ahead of time—she would just hope to see her at the show tonight.

Talk coming from a corner of the post office got her attention as she reached to open the door. They were talking about a shooting at a bank this morning. She caught snatches of the conversation.

"Deppity Ranger was in the bank when they tried

to rob it. There was two of 'em and only one of him, but he shot 'em both to doll rags. They didn't have no chance."

The crowd was pressing around an old man who was obviously enjoying the attention. He checked his audience and went on.

"Hadn't been a Ranger no more'n about day or two, that's what I heard him tell the sheriff. They made us leave afore I could hear the rest. Dangdest thing I ever saw...one feller was a-takin' the cash from the teller when this Ranger walked in, hauled iron and shot him twice. Mebbe three times. Happened so fast, I can't remember. Feller never got a shot off."

The old man checked his audience and kept going. "Didn't sound like no Texan when he talked. Mebbe from somewhere up in the hills. Tennessee or Kentucky or somewhere. Anyway, the second robber come runnin' out from the vault and this feller dropped him with one shot. Right through the heart. Dead as Caesar, right there. Had one of them new Colts, they said."

Victoria turned and pressed through the crowd to listen. The old man came up for air. "What was his name?" she asked anxiously. "The Ranger, I mean. Did you hear his name?"

The old man shook his head. "Didn't get no name, miss. Tall, rangy feller, dark hair. Young man. Kinda handsome, I guess you could say."

Victoria pulled back and let the crowd press around the storyteller. She hurried down the street, her mind full of questions. She'd not heard Nash say anything about being a Ranger. Just that he might take a bounty hunting job that would bring him to Austin. There must be others who were Rangers and would fit that description. Still, though, she found herself wondering. And she had to admit she was a bit worried.

# Chapter 9
## *Murph's Warning*

A funny thing happened on my way to see Victoria at her show in Austin. I was hustling down Congress Avenue, thinking about two things. One, I didn't have just a whole lot of time to get to the show early enough for a front-row seat. And two, I'm not a man who gets a lot of new ideas. I'm talking about how the roses had worked for me the first time. Actually, that was Charles Goodnight's idea. I needed to get some more flowers before the show, on account of I couldn't think of anything else.

Both ideas kinda went up in smoke when I heard my name bein' called out from somewhere behind me.

"Nash!" somebody yelled. "Nash Walker!"

I turned around and saw a guy with a badge trotting in my direction. He didn't have to get close enough for a good look at his face before I knew who it was—Murph, the Texas Ranger I had met up in Georgetown. For a man shaped like a barrel, I thought, he was picking them feet up and puttin' 'em down. He got to me in no time. He was sucking a little air when he got there, though.

He took off his hat and wiped off his forehead. "Ain't you something?" he bellowed, clapping me on the shoulder. "You ain't been in Austin more than a day, and you already sent two bank robbers to Boot Hill!"

My mouth worked open and shut a few times, but there weren't no words coming out that I can recall. I must have looked like a fish on the bottom of a boat.

Murph chuckled. "Word gets around," he said. "Especially when we'd all been told to be on the lookout for those boys. Don't worry none, you did us all a favor." He clapped his hat back on his head and pointed across the street. "Let's go over to that diner and have us a cup of coffee. There are a couple of things I want to talk to you about."

I got a little antsy along about then, shifting from one foot to the other, takin' a peek at the sun dropping in the west, wondering if I had time to get a few flowers and a front-row seat at the show.

"Don't worry," he said, leading the way across the street. "You'll have lots 'o time to get a ticket to that show."

I looked at him sideways and he chuckled again. "Levi told me I could find you right around here, trying to get to that show. He said you like the juggler."

I growled to myself and followed Murph across the street. That Levi, he had him a big mouth.

We taken a seat in the diner. *Took a seat,* I corrected myself. I had to quit talkin' like I'd come straight down out of the Tennessee hills yesterday. I reminded myself I'd had two job offers today already, so I must be doing something right.

Murph told the waiter to bring some coffee and I did the same, even though I don't much like coffee after breakfast time. I'd had a few beers at the saloon and I didn't need any more beer. I was out to make another good impression tonight. I squinted across the table at Murph and waited.

"First," he said, "Leander McNelly told me he'd like it if you joined up with the special company he's gettin' outfitted." He stirred his coffee and stared across the table. "That is a big honor. Lots of the boys would like to join that outfit. You must have impressed McNelly. That ain't easy to do."

I just nodded, and Murph shrugged. "He said you wasn't ready to join up with him right now, but you can come and see me if'n you change your mind." I nodded again.

"That brings me to the other thing," Murph said. "Levi said you were maybe goin' to go to work for the Taylor outfit. Cattle folks. Big outfit east of here."

I decided it was time to actually say something and not just sit there and nod. "I saw a guy I knew in the Army earlier today," I explained. "He remembered me from the war, said he works for a big cattle outfit named Taylor Ranch, said he could teach me how to be a rancher. I ain't said yes, but I'm thinking I'll go."

Murph stared out the window. He kept stirring the coffee. "What's that guy's name?" he asked suddenly. "The one from the Army? Did you remember him?"

"Shadrach Taylor. He said they called him Shade." I shrugged. "Maybe I remember him. There was a lot going on there at Shiloh. He knew which outfit I was in."

Murph kept looking out the window. I think he was

trying to decide if he'd heard that name. Finally, he just shrugged and took a slurp at his coffee. I was guessing he didn't know the name or he would have said so. I didn't know if that was good or bad.

"Okay," he said, pushing the coffee away. "I'll just put my cards on the table and tell you what I know about the Taylor outfit. Might be a good deal for you to work for them. Maybe not. You kin decide."

He leaned his elbows on the table. "The Taylor outfit is a big'un," he agreed. "There's been a little bad blood betwixt those boys and another outfit called Sutton. Mostly, they've both just got family workin' for them there, but a few hardcases seem to have drifted out that way. Maybe it'll settle down, maybe not. If it don't settle down, there could be a shootin' war." He shrugged again. "Maybe not."

He had my attention. I waited.

"The Taylor outfit—one of the main family members that got it started was named Billy Taylor. There was word goin' around that ole Billy Taylor dropped a loop over cows that wasn't his now and then. Got a little careless with the branding iron." He waited.

"Rustling," I said.

"That's what they say. I didn't see it myself. Anyway, old Billy Taylor got hisself shot and kilt last year, and there's been some bad blood about it. Folks are waiting to see if the Suttons stop some lead if the Taylors decide to get even."

Murph waved for another coffee and kept going. "There's one of the Suttons named Bob Sutton, who was a Texas Ranger for a while. Now he's one of the folks who owns that big Sutton outfit. Some folks called him Bad Bob Sutton when he was with us. I never rode with Bob, but there's folks that did who tell me Bob shot first and thought things over later. He wouldn't exackly be a peacemaker, is what I'm sayin'."

"Range war," I mumbled. Even up there in Tennessee, I'd heard of range wars.

Murph shrugged one more time. "Maybe it'll happen, maybe not. Sometimes folks just cool off and come to their senses. I thought you should have your eyes open if you go out there." He studied me over his coffee cup. "Good pay, they say the grub's good and the work ain't too hard."

He put the coffee cup down. "Do they think you might be a gun hand for them?"

That's the thought I'd been chasing around in the back of my head. "I don't know," I admitted. "I'm wondering now if Shade Taylor maybe had already heard about the shootin' at the bank this morning. You sure found out in a hurry."

Murph leaned back and went back to looking out the window. "I'm askin' one thing," he said, "as a favor. If you think there's a shootin' war shaping up out there, or somebody getting even for Billy Taylor, I'm asking you to come and tell me about it. I want to keep from spilling blood if I can."

That made sense to me. The blood I'd spilled in the war and again here in Texas was more than enough for me. I held out my hand across the table. "Deal," I said.

We shook hands and I left, heading for the show again. I didn't have time to stop for any flowers, but when I cut across something they called Republic Square, I saw some flowers growing here and there. I stopped and picked some kind of flower. I'm not sure what it was, but I tucked it inside my jacket and kept going.

When I got to the opera house, there weren't any tickets in the front row. I wasn't expecting any, so I just got the best seat I could and settled in. The jokes weren't as funny as the first time anymore, but I still enjoyed myself and waited for Victoria's songs. She sounded every bit as good as the first time. The show was over before I knew it.

Now I had to figure out where I could go to make sure I saw her when she came out. I walked out to the lobby and got the lay of the land. It looked like there was a hallway coming from the back and out here to the lobby. There were just a few folks standing there like they were waiting for somebody, so I joined them. I didn't see any other way for the performers to come out.

Waiting outside that hall was a lady in a faded brown dress, looking like she'd stepped off a farm some-where, with an older man who looked like he was with her. He gave me a sharp look and nodded. He looked older than my pa would be if he'd survived the war, but I wouldn't tangle with this guy, old or not. He had seen some fights and smelled some gun smoke in his day, I'd wager.

I pulled the flower out of my jacket and waited. The lady in the brown dress looked at me and smiled. "You brought a flower for somebody," she said. "Some-body in the show?"

I stared at my boots and cleared my throat a couple times. "Yes, ma'am," I finally told her. "The lady that sings *Clementine* and *Home on the Range*, she surely sings like an angel. These are for her, if'n I can find her. She ain't...isn't expecting me, I reckon."

The lady's mouth dropped wide open, and her smile got twice as wide. Just then, Victoria came through the door. "Mom!" she exclaimed, then gave the lady in the brown dress a hug. Then she walked over, took the flower, and gave me a kiss on the cheek. "Nash!" she said. "You've met my mother!"

\* \* \*

We got to talking and Victoria's mother, Margie, said she was going to buy us all dinner and wouldn't hear anything else about it. I protested that I could pay, but Victoria leaned over and told me not to worry about it. We walked back down to the same diner where I had been with Murph before the show.

Victoria and her mom talked about things at the ranch. The man with the white hair said his name was Alec. The two of us mostly put our food down the hatch where it belonged while the ladies talked. Then Margie, about halfway through a sentence, grabbed Victoria's arm and stared across the table at me.

"We heard about bank robbers!" she gasped. "Right here in Austin. A temporary Texas Ranger with a new kind of gun shot them both, that's what we heard!"

I thought about my badge, which was tucked away in my pocket. Alec was carrying an older Navy Colt on his hip, but I had my brand-new Army Colt on mine. Victoria looked at me across the table, and I got a feeling she knew it was me. Alec saw the look, glanced down at my new Colt, then went on eating. When Margie finished with her story, Victoria said the two of 'em were going to excuse themselves for a minute. I remembered my manners just in time and stood when they went out. Victoria gave me another long look across the table and left.

Alec reached to cut another piece of bread and offered me one. He looked down at my pistol again and nodded at me. "You done what you had to," was all he said. I relaxed and finished the dinner with them. Alec said nothing else the whole meal.

Standing outside the café after dinner, it turned out that Victoria and her mother were staying in hotels in the opposite direction from each other. Margie took over. "Alec is staying at the same place as me. He'll walk me over."

She stepped over and gave Victoria a hug. "You come on home and see us when you can," she told Victoria. She gave me a hug as well. "You watch out for her," she said.

"Yes, ma'am," I promised. "All she has to do is holler and I'll come a-foggin...I'll come runnin'." I glanced over at Victoria. She seemed to be grinning at the boardwalk.

Margie chuckled. "You just feel free to come a-foggin' it if she calls, Nash Walker," she grinned. Then she left with Alec, walking the other way down Fourth Street.

We strolled down Fourth Street, took a turn, and stopped outside her hotel. Victoria stepped up on the first step and took my face in both hands. "Tell me about the bank robbers this morning," she said. "Something tells me that was you in the bank, a temporary Texas Ranger with a new six-shot Colt."

Well sir, that had taken me aback. "Your ma heard

all that before dinner," I said. I shook my head. I was used to the hills of Tennessee. It would have taken two weeks of talkin' at the feed store or barbershop to pass that news around back home.

So, I started at the beginning, back when I walked over to the bank and stepped into the shootout. I told her about shooting the robbers, how it was them or me, and how hard it still was to believe it had happened.

From there, I went on to tell her about my old Army buddy Shade Taylor, and how Leander McNelly had come to see me and both had offered jobs. I threw in how I was still thinking about getting some cows and going to Denver with Charles Goodnight. I'm not sure how long it took me to run out of steam. I finally just quit talking.

Victoria backed up a step, watching me run down and out of words. "Well," she finally said, "you've been even busier than I thought. You didn't get hurt this morning? Not even a scratch?"

I shook my head. "Seemed like there was plenty of bullets flyin' around," I admitted. "But none of 'em found me."

"Okay." Victoria stayed on the top step, trying to remember what she had heard about the Taylor and Sutton ranches. They weren't too far from their home ranch, and she knew those families didn't get along. She couldn't remember much else.

"Which one of those jobs do you want to do?" she asked. The job at the Taylor ranch was likely to keep him closer to Austin, she thought, and that was nice, but she didn't even know how long she would be in this town herself.

I stared at the hotel door behind her, trying to

decide. I knew I didn't have much time to make up my mind. "I don't wanna join the Rangers. Not right now, anyway. I've done enough shootin' and getting shot at for right now."

I sorted through the thoughts running around in my brain. "I'd like to make that drive with Goodnight," I admitted. "But right now I don't have enough money to buy cows and I don't know much about cowboyin'. I think maybe the thing to do right now is go out and take the ranch job. There's a lot I could learn and I could save up some more money."

"That makes sense," she told me. She stepped forward and gave me another kiss on the cheek. I was liking those kisses on the cheek. She stepped inside and disappeared into the hotel. I turned around and headed for my boarding house. I would find Levi in the morning and tell him what I was doing, then I would find the Taylor ranch and look up Shadrach Taylor.

\* \* \*

It was a little past first light when I roused myself out of the bed at the boardinghouse, loaded up my bag and checked out with the clerk. It was early, but not too early to find Levi down at the diner, where I knew he was likely to go for breakfast.

I was on my second cup of coffee when he strolled through the door, waved, and walked over to straddle the chair across the table. He waved for a coffee and studied the menu. "Eggs and bacon," he told the waiter. "Lots of 'em."

He nodded at my horse at the hitching rail right

outside the window. "Looks like you're all loaded up to go, Pard," he said. "Which job you gonna take?"

"Taylor Ranch," I said. "I'll save me up a little money, then make that drive with Goodnight up to Denver and give myself a good stake for whatever I want to do. I'll have to think about what I want to do after that. I'm not ready for anything else right now."

"Good plan," he agreed. "Watch yourself out there at the Taylor place," he warned. "They've got themselves some differences. They might settle 'em peaceful, or they might not. Don't tell anybody yore business that don't need to know. You don't know who's friends and who's enemies out there. No need to take sides. Be best if they don't know you've been a Ranger."

Levi waved his coffee cup in the air for a refill. "You were Army buddies with this guy Shadrach, right?"

I shook my head. "Not sure if I remember him," I admitted. "They ain't much on first names in the Army, so I guess they just called him Taylor. I'd likely remember a name like Shadrach."

The part about not saying much about myself sounded like a good idea. "Murph said the same thing— said to keep my yap shut about myself," I told him. "He also told me to let him know if there's a shooting war about to break out."

Levi stopped with a forkful of eggs halfway to his mouth. "Well," he drawled. "If you tell the Rangers, don't show up again at either ranch after you do. No tellin' who might take a shot at you if you bring in the law."

"Okay, that makes sense." I finished up my breakfast, said my goodbyes, straddled Cisco, and headed him east, out of town. I was wondering if this was one of

those times I needed to think things over a little more
before I jumped in. I shrugged and stopped thinking
about it. I was just going to learn some things about
cowboyin'. Roping and riding herd seemed easy
enough. I would just mind my own business and save a
few dollars. That was my play, anyway.

# Chapter 10
## *Taylor Ranch*

It was a day's ride to the Taylor Ranch, from what I'd been told. I got a map drawn up by the guy that owned the general store. That was the least he could do for me —I'd already bought my new Colt and had an order with him for the Winchester 73. I figure I was just about the only customer he needed. Add in Levi's orders, and he was set for the next year.

Daybreak saw me saddled up with a belly full of biscuits, riding east toward the rising sun and the Taylor Ranch. I didn't mind it taking all day. If I rode in about the time they sounded the dinner bell, that was okay with me. I had already asked Shadrach *Shade* Taylor if he was kin to the Taylors that owned the ranch, but he said no.

After a couple hours, the landscape flattened out a little, going from hilly country to rolling grassy meadows and stands of post oaks. When we crossed the Colorado River, I stopped on the far bank to water Cisco.

The storekeep had warned me to watch out for

snakes. Diamondback rattlers and copperheads were the two he mentioned that got my attention. We had timber rattlers in Tennessee. I didn't think I'd like the diamondbacks any better than their cousins. I kept my ears open for any rattling sounds, then settled myself down against a tree and chewed on some jerky. Kept one eye open, too.

I knew there were a couple of Indian tribes out this way, but I'd heard they were peaceful. Caddos and some Kickapoos was what Levi had told me. I kept the other eye open for Indians that didn't look peaceful.

I passed some small cattle outfits along the way. They were friendly, with the cowboys waving at me. I waved back and kept moving. Things changed in the late afternoon. I'd struck a trail that should take me where I was going, according to my map. The afternoon sun was warm on my back when I saw three riders kicking up dust on the trail, headed my way. Being a naturally cautious man, I pulled my Henry rifle from the scabbard and laid it across my lap.

They fanned out across the trail as they got closer. I reined in Cisco and backed him around a little to get some trees at my back. When the first rider moved to flank me on the right, I let the muzzle of the Henry follow him.

They reined in and stared at me. The one in the middle looked like the old bull of the woods to me. Thick, wavy gray hair and a nasty scar on the left cheek. They all waited and glanced sideways at me. The old bull of the woods stared, looking me up and down, then nudged his horse forward.

"That's a nice-lookin' smokewagon you got there,"

he said, looking at my Colt. He pushed his horse forward another step. "You any good with that thang?"

I slid my right hand over, stopping about two inches away from the Colt. "Just one way to find out that I know of," I said, locking eyes with him.

He stopped and studied me with some hard eyes. I glanced over at the brand on his horse. It was a Lazy S. Sutton outfit, I figured. He kept staring at me. His eyes seemed just a tad too close together.

"He's blowin' smoke, Uncle Bob." This came from that anxious young pup on my right. I nudged the Henry to lay the muzzle right on his chest. He sucked in a little air and shut up.

The old bull of the woods was still watching me. "You workin' around here?" he asked, studying my guns some more. "I ain't seen you around these parts."

"Just passin' through," I said.

"Hmmmph." He looked at the Colt again. "I'll not try you," he decided. He waved at the other two. "Let's go, boys." The young pup on my right opened his yap to protest, then shut it down after one look at Uncle Bob.

I moved Cisco just slightly to keep 'em in my sight as they rode past. When they disappeared around a bend in the trail, I urged Cisco forward. I still had time to catch the dinner bell. I'd say nothing about this when I got to the Taylor Ranch. I had a feeling I had just met old Bad Bob Sutton. He had at least one nephew that was looking to put a notch or two on his gun. I didn't aim to be one of the notches.

I met nobody else on my way to the Taylor Ranch. I knew it when I found it. It was a big spread with more cows than I'd seen in one place in my life. There was a path turning off the trail with a big arch overhead. They had burned the letters *TR* into the arch. I took that to be the Taylor brand. Cisco and me moved on down the path. I was trying to decide if I should ask for Shadrach or Shade when I got there.

It turned out he found me. The cook was ringing the triangle on the back porch and serving up huge helpings of beef stew and cornbread when I rode up. I turned my horse into the corral along with a couple of other guys, and nobody questioned me, which I thought was a little funny.

I grabbed a bowl and got into the chow line. Nobody paid much attention to me. I noticed four guys a little off to themselves. Folks seemed to step aside and let them get in the front of the line. They went off by themselves with the food, spurs clinking and double pistols on their hips. Everybody seemed glad enough to let them go.

Cook stared at me when I got to the front of the line. "New here?" he asked, working a toothpick around in his mouth.

I stared back. "Yup. A guy named Shade said I could come."

Cook shrugged and put a steaming cup of stew in my bowl. He pointed at the cornbread, and I took a hunk of that along with a slab of butter. I took a seat by myself on the steps of the back porch of the ranch house and was about halfway to the bottom of the bowl when I heard my name.

"Nash! Nash Walker!"

It was Shade Taylor, along with a guy I didn't know. Shade pumped my hand and pointed to the other man. "JW Hardin," he said.

Hardin looked like he didn't care who I was. He

shook my hand once and moved off to the food line without saying anything. I saw him take his food and go down the path where the four hardcases with double-tied-down guns had gone.

Shade went to get some food and joined me on the back steps. "Glad yore here," he boomed. "Got lotsa work for you to do." He barked out a few names, and men came over to meet me. Shade pointed out one in particular.

"Curly," he said, pointing at a guy who was completely bald.

Curly grinned and rubbed a hand over his scalp. "Used to be curly," he explained. "Name stuck. Better'n Baldy."

"Nash, here, is new," Shade proclaimed. "Knew him in the war. He don't know ropin' and herdin' and such, but he'll work hard. Good man. You can teach him what he needs to know, right, Curly?"

Curly shot me a quick glance and nodded. "Hard workers, I got no problem with. Find me in the mornin' and we'll get you started."

Shade stayed with me on the porch. "Watch this," he told me. "Hey, Cookie!" he blurted. I watched him walk over and slip a coin to the cook. Shade followed him inside and came back out a minute later with two huge slabs of apple pie.

"It pays to know Cookie." He grinned.

We finished off the pie, and Shade pointed out the bunkhouse to me. "Take any cot that's open," he said. "If the sheets ain't messed up and there's no junk under the cot, it's open."

I started off to check the bunkhouse when Shade called out to me one more time.

"Nash," he said. "They told me in town you was wearin' a Ranger's badge when you shot them boys in the bank. You done bein' a Ranger? They said you was temporary."

"Done." I nodded, wondering why he cared about that.

"Good." He nodded. "Bein' good with a gun is a handy thing in Texas. I can work with you if ya want, teach how to draw and move quick, how to handle yourself even better if'n you get in another scrape."

"Okay." I moved on toward the bunkhouse, trying to sort a few things out in my head. It looked like a nice place. Great food, and I thought I could work for Curly, no problem. I wondered, though, about what Shade had just said, and about the four guys who looked like gunhands, and about JW Hardin. Everybody seemed to walk a wide path around him.

*  *  *

Curly settled down on the bench next to me just as I was tucking into a big breakfast of flapjacks and bacon. He plunked down his own breakfast and a second cup of coffee for me. He glanced sideways.

"Well, don't nobody have to teach you about eatin'," he observed. "How about riding hosses? I know you ain't done any roping or herdin', but it'll help if you have ridden some hosses." He glanced out into the corral. "They told me you've got a good 'un."

"Yep," I said. "I rode with the cavalry during the war. Three years on horseback, ridin' all the time."

Curly nodded. "Whose unit?"

"Forrest," I said. "Nathan Bedford Forrest. We just

about lived in the saddle. Had some long days just seein' the world from between a hosses' ears."

"Okay," Curly agreed. "You can ride. That'll help. There are times when you need both yore hands for the rope. You'll have to guide the hoss with yore knees and keep yore seat in the leather. I won't worry about that part. Finish breakfast an' I'll get you started with tying the loop and tossin' the rope."

We spent the morning doing what Curly said. Tying the knot and getting the lasso set wasn't that hard. Curly said I had a pretty good feel for tossing the rope. I don't know about that part. He had me throwing at a fencepost, and I missed it as much as I hit it. And the post wasn't even moving.

When it was getting closer to lunchtime, we left off roping the post and saddled up. Curly took me to a good-sized corral that had about ten calves kickin' up their heels and running around. He shook out a loop.

"Watch me for a bit an' watch the calves," he told me. "Watch how they like to duck their heads and dodge when I throw the rope. And," he said, shaking his finger, "don't never forget to wrap that rope around your saddle horn jest as soon as you throw it. You get yourself tied in to a big calf without doing that and you'll land on yore noggin' the corral before you know it."

I watched for about a half hour, and the calves did just like he said, ducking their heads and dodging. Even Curly missed a few, but he got more than he missed. We called it off when Cookie rang the triangle on the back porch for lunch.

"We'll work for mebbe an hour more after lunch," Curly told me. "You kin take a turn with the lasso and get the hang of it a little better. After that, I've got to help move a herd to a better pasture out there. We'll see if Shade had something else for you to do this afternoon."

Shade showed up just about the time I was finishing lunch. I noticed he came in with JW Hardin, who grabbed some lunch and disappeared into the bunkhouse. Shade came over to join Curly and me, then came with us as I saddled up Cisco and went to try my luck roping the calves.

After a while, I was doing about as well with the calves as I had done on the fencepost, which I thought was pretty good progress. I swung a wide loop and tried to cover 'em whichever way they swung their head or dodged. I tightened up the rope right away when they ducked their heads and cinched the rope around my saddle horn. Even Cisco started to get the hang of things, backing up to tighten the rope.

Curly called a halt, and I thought maybe he was grinning a little. "We'll let you try tomorrow on bigger calves and mebbe a cow or two," he said. "If you get the hang of that, we'll let you join us bustin' the brush to round up runaways." There was a twinkle in his eye when he said, I'm pretty sure.

He rode off to move a herd and left me there with Shade, who didn't seem all that interested in how I was doing with the roping. He eyed my new Army Colt. I noticed his guns were the older Navy Colt, but he had both of 'em on now. In town, he'd worn only one. One holster had been empty, though.

He rode over closer to me. "Kin I have a look at that new Colt?" He was already reaching for it. I gave it to him.

Shade spun the cylinder and sighted down the

barrel, testing the weight of it. "Nice," was all he said at first. He handed it back. "How fast can you reload that thang?"

I thought about the morning in the bank. It had seemed like a long time, thumbing those cartridges in the cylinder and looking up and down for the one robber still in the vault. After a while, I shrugged. "Maybe a minute or two," I said, "by the time I get them cartridges out of my belt and into the gun."

He led me out of the corral and across a pasture into a stand of post oak trees. There was a fallen log on the ground, stretching out about twenty feet. He laid six empty cans on the log. "Have you drawn it and shot as fast as you can?" he asked.

I thought back to my sessions with Levi Noone. "Some," I said. "I didn't do much of that in the Army," I admitted.

He started by telling me to draw at my own speed and shoot the cans. That was pretty easy. I knocked down all six on the first try. After that, he had me draw and shoot, going faster and faster. Once or twice, he pointed out that I needed to be sure to clear the holster before I tried to come level.

After several reloads and a lot of wasted ammo, he called a halt to it. "You're fast," he said, staring at the gun again. "Surprising fast. Pretty danged accurate. Be sure you clear that leather. Don't be afraid to crouch down a little to steady yourself if that helps."

He walked back over, set up some new cans, then came back. He turned, drew, and fired six times, knocking 'em all over on the first try. I noticed he crouched a little and moved to his right as he went. I filed that away in my brain. He was really fast and hit 'em all. I wondered how many gunfights he'd been in. Moving to his right probably took him out of the line of fire. That could be a handy thing to know.

We mounted up and moved back toward the ranch. "You can take the rest of the day to settle in," he said. "You jest barely got here in time to look things over yesterday. Mr. Taylor is gone today, but I'll introduce you tomorrow."

We parted ways at the corral. "Help Cookie with dinner if you want." He grinned. "I'll bet there's more of that apple pie you got yesterday."

I unsaddled Cisco and brushed him down. I could see Shade move off toward the bunkhouse and go inside. A few minutes later, he came out with JW Hardin. They mounted up and rode out, moving north and away from the ranch house.

I found a place to store my saddle in the barn and left Cisco in the corral. Shade seemed more interested in my gun skills than my cowboying skills. That troubled me some. On the other hand, I figured I could learn a lot from Curly.

Nobody was there in the clubhouse. I decided to take Shade's advice about helping Curly. Maybe there was some apple pie left over from yesterday.

* * *

Shadrach *Shade* Taylor and JW Hardin rode steadily until they reined in at the crest of a hill, watching Sutton cattle grazing in the valley stretching away to the north.

"How many cowboys they got watchin' this herd?" Shade Taylor asked.

Hardin took a minute to light a cigar, then shrugged. "Only two cowboys, mebbe a hunnerd head of cattle," he answered. "If the cowboys don't give us no trouble and keep their mouths shut, the Suttons won't miss them cows for a long time."

Shade Taylor nodded. He didn't need to ask what would happen if the cowboys gave them trouble.

Hardin finished setting an even fire to the tip of the cigar, then sucked in a lungful of smoke. "Is that new boy, Walker, ready to help us?" he asked.

Shade shrugged. "Don't know. He's good with the gun, real good. Ain't never seen him in action with somebody shootin' back, but they say he handled things in that bank. We can ease him in slow, give him some easy money."

Hardin leaned over the saddle and spit. "He was workin' for the Rangers, though. That's what you said."

Shade nodded and shrugged again. "Lotsa guys have worked both sides of the law. We've both seen that. If he don't wanna join us, there ain't nobody out there in this world gonna miss him."

# Chapter 11
## *Night Ride*

Early morning found me joining up with Curly for some roping practice on a few cows that he was planning to move back toward the main herd. We found two heifers grazing along a creek bottom. Curly showed me how to move behind them and push them out. We let out a few yips and whistles to get them moving up the bank and out to the pasture.

"Shake out a loop and give roping 'em a try," Curly hollered. "Don't forget to wrap that rope around the saddle horn."

I did as he said, moving up to cut off one heifer as she tried to get back to the creek bottom. I tossed the first lasso and missed when she ducked down and away. I pulled the rope back in and tossed at the second cow, figuring she would do the same again.

Curly grinned and pumped his fist in the air when I got the second one. He had me rope the heifers a couple more times as we moved them back to the main herd. When those two had joined the others, Curly had an announcement for me.

"You're gonna come with us to do a little brush-poppin' tomorrow," he told me.

I stared at him. "What's brush-poppin'?"

He grinned. "We get us a few strays that wander out into some thick brush, thorns and such. We have to move 'em out and get them back to the main herd." He stopped and looked at what I was wearing.

"Well, you've got yoreself a nice, wide-brimmed hat, good boots, long sleeves on your shirt." He looked down at my pants. "Canvas pants," he mumbled. "We'll have to get you some chaps. Like these." He pointed at the tough leather coverings for his pants. "Gonna need a little more protection in them thickets." He looked at my neck. "We'll get you a bandana, too."

"Okay. You got something that'll fit?"

Curly chuckled. "Well, you're a long, tall fella, so they might be a little short. That won't matter. They'll cover you down to yore boots."

I followed him back to the ranch house after we had met two other cowboys and checked the herd. Curly pronounced the cows in good shape and gave me some tips on checking the herd for injured or sick animals.

When we got back to the ranch house, Curly whistled to get my attention as I was heading for the chow line. I looked over to see him standing there with Shade and somebody I hadn't seen before.

As I approached, Curly pointed at the guy I didn't know. "Creed Taylor," he said. "Creed is the boss-man around here."

Creed Taylor glanced at me and shook my hand. "I'm no kin to Shadrach here," he explained, "but Shade says you're good people. Welcome. What are you doing so far?"

"Just learning from Curly," I began.

Curly chuckled. "He's gonna come brush-poppin' with us tomorrow. We've got us a few strays off to the east."

Creed Taylor nodded, looked at the Colt on my hip, then glanced over at Shade.

"After Curly is done with him, we'll take him up north with us and bring back a couple hundred head that strayed off," Shade told him.

Creed met his eyes, nodded briefly, then turned on his heel and walked off.

I wandered on over to the dinner line, thinking there was something a little strange about that last part. Maybe I was imagining things. Why had he checked my gun, then left just as soon as Shade talked about a stray herd? It was almost like the boss didn't want to hear anything more about it.

I shrugged and grabbed a plate. Beef and beans tonight. I could live with that.

* * *

We were up at daybreak. Cookie grumbled a lot, but he got a little breakfast together for us, along with jerky and biscuits for lunch. Curly introduced me to three others named Large, Shorty, and Louie. I didn't have to ask how Large got his name. I would have named him Huge.

Curly led a short, tough-looking mustang. "This here's Mouse," he told me. "You don't wanna let that nice horse of yours loose in all that brush and stickers. Mouse here is just what you need." Mouse flared his nostrils and rolled a glassy eyeball at me.

"We're gonna get along," I told Mouse. I wasn't so sure.

We rode about an hour due south until I could see the brush and stickers Curly had been telling me about. We topped a low rise and saw at least a dozen cows spread out in the brush. Curly formed us into a line, and we moved forward, yipping and clucking at them.

We cleared out the first valley without too much trouble. I was glad for the chaps and gloves Curly had given me. Brush and stickers clawed at me with every step. We pushed the thirteen head we had rounded up down to a stream in the bottom of the next valley and left Shorty to keep them together.

The next cows we came across were together in the bottom of a low gully running through the middle of a pasture. There were eighteen of them down there, and the brush was thicker and higher. The three of us formed a line and started pushing them through. The morning was heating up, and sweat rolled down my cheeks as I cut back and forth, keeping them in front of me. I had to admit, Mouse knew what he was doing. He had him a mean streak that was coming in handy when the cows tried to break away.

There was a little mossy-horned steer in front of me now, and he kept trying to make a break back into the brush. Mouse was faster and nimbler, but the steer made us work. I could hear Large and Curly whistling and yipping to get the last of 'em through the brush when old Mossy-Horn made a break for it.

He bolted through the last of the brush on my right, then cut hard farther to the right, trying to get around and behind me. The brush and stickers cut through my shirt sleeves as I urged Mouse on through and shook out a loop before the steer could get away.

It was now or never. I threw the lasso, banking on him ducking and dodging to the right to get past me. Maybe it was luck, but that loop settled over his head, nice as you please. Like I said, it might have been luck, but I pulled him up tight and wrapped the rope around my saddle horn. Mouse skidded to a stop and pulled him up short.

I tried not to let on how pleased I was with myself when I led the steer over to join the other cows we had pushed out of that brush. The rest of the day was just as hot, sweaty and hard, but I was holding my own.

By the time we'd finished, we had fifty cows, all wearing the TR brand, to show for our troubles. My shirt was pretty tore up by the time we got back to the ranch. Large cast an eye in my direction and offered a little advice as I led Mouse into the corral.

"Git yoreself a denim shirt," he advised. "It'll hold up better to them stickers and brush next time."

I settled in with my chow at dinner, checking over all the scratches on my arms. The bandana Curly had given me was all torn up, as well as my shirt. I stuffed the bandana into my pocket. The chaps he'd given me, though, were the best thing I'd seen since moonshine. Maybe even better than moonshine. They'd held up to all the scratching and all the sharp sticks and branches all day long.

I was thinking maybe I had earned myself an easy day mending fences or something, but that idea didn't last when Shade showed up and plopped himself down next to me.

"In the mornin'," he said, "we've got to go and get a

little herd that wandered off up north. They don't have to be rounded up," he assured me. "They're just grazin' near some water. Mebbe two hours north. We've got a few thangs to do first, so you help Curly some more in the mornin'. We'll leave mid-afternoon and drive 'em back to the ranch by dark."

That sounded pretty late to me, but Shade didn't look like he wanted to hear any questions about that. "Who's goin'?" was all I asked.

"Just us and them boys," he said, pointing. I looked over where he was pointing. It was JW Hardin and the four guys that looked like gunhands to me. Why, I wondered, would we need that many guys for a little herd?

\* \* \*

Victoria entered the café, looking for her usual breakfast. The shows went fairly late into the evening, so her reward for herself was a leisurely morning and a good breakfast at this café. Her mother and Alec had left earlier this morning, so she had nothing to do until a meeting for the performers in the late afternoon.

A waitress hurried over to seat her, but her attention was caught by a short, stocky man wearing a badge. He was seated at a table in the corner. There was a taller, dark-haired man in nice clothes sitting across the table.

She knew, from Nash's description, that the guy wearing the Texas Rangers badge had to be Murph. Nash had described him perfectly. She wasn't sure about the other man, but he looked to be a businessman. A successful one, to judge by his appearance.

The waitress reached her and pointed toward an empty table, but Victoria held her hand in the air to stop her.

She pointed toward Murph. "Could you give me just a minute to ask this man a question?" she asked.

The waitress stepped back and nodded. Victoria moved toward the table in the corner. Both men stood when she reached the table.

"Sorry," she said, "I didn't want to interrupt you gentlemen." Her gaze settled on the Ranger. "You just have to be Murph," she said. "My friend Nash Walker described you perfectly. Can I ask you a question about the place where he's gone to take a job—the Taylor Ranch?"

Murph pulled out an empty chair and motioned for her to sit down. He brushed aside her objections about interrupting them. "I'm glad to answer your questions, miss," he said. "And my friend here, Mr. Goodnight, might be able to help you, too."

Victoria glanced at the other man in surprise. "Charles Goodnight!" she said. "I think you know Nash Walker as well."

Goodnight smiled just briefly and nodded his head. "Did he take my tip and bring you flowers?" he asked. "I'm guessing you're the lady that sings in the show."

Victoria broke into a grin. She knew she must be blushing just a little. "He did," she murmured. "I loved those flowers."

Murph shot a glance between the two of them. "Maybe that's where he was in such a hurry to go the other night," he said, half to himself. He turned his attention to Victoria. "You want to know about the Taylor place," he said. "What do you need to know?"

"Is it safe for him to be there?" she blurted. She stopped and tried to explain. "My family is in ranching," she said, "and we've heard a few things about the Taylors and Suttons not getting along. Is Nash in danger?"

Murph and Goodnight exchanged a long look. Murph nodded unhappily. "Things ain't real smooth out there, from what I hear," he agreed. "I talked to Nash so's he'll have some idea of what he's gettin' into. I told him to come and find me if he sees trouble."

Victoria frowned at the table, then looked at Murph. "Do you think he'll be able to get away and come here? If there's trouble, I mean."

Murph and Goodnight exchanged a look. Murph still looked troubled. Goodnight leaned forward.

"I'm going out there," he told Victoria. "I'll be talking to Creed Taylor about buying some cattle. I'll make sure to look up Nash while I'm at the ranch. If there's trouble, I'll find a way to get him out of there."

Victoria watched his face and felt comfortable Goodnight was going to keep his promise. She smiled and rose from the table. "Thank you," she told them both. She looked back at Goodnight. "And thank you for the flower suggestion." She chuckled. She headed for her table to order breakfast.

* * *

I spent the morning on fence repair. Curly said he was going to give me a break on the roping and herding today. He said to check in with Shade at lunchtime about rounding up and driving in the herd that had wandered up north.

I'd had a few worries about what JW Hardin and Shade were up to, but I managed to start feeling better about it by the time I came in for lunch. I started to worry about it again when Shade and JW Hardin came my way in the lunch line.

"You got enough to keep you busy for a few hours this afternoon?" Shade asked.

I nodded. "There's a few hours' work left mending those fences," I told him.

"Good," he said. "Come on down to the corral in maybe three hours and we'll be ready to go. We've got a couple horses that still need shoein' before we can go."

I watched Shade and Hardin walking away, wondering just how long it would take for us to reach those cows up north. Any more than two or three hours and we would be working in the dark. Not only was that gonna be harder, it started to sound like cattle rustling. Even a cowboy tenderfoot like me knew that rustling was best done after dark.

I wandered over to Curly and stopped him feeding his face long enough to ask a question. "I've heard about a big Sutton outfit around here," I said, trying to sound as casual as I could. "What direction are they from where we are right now?"

Curly's head came up when I said the word Sutton, and he looked both directions before he answered. "North," he said, taking a sharp look at me. "You'll wanna stay away from those boys."

"Right." I waved a hand carelessly and walked away. *Nash, boy*, I told myself, *you're gonna have to step careful*.

As it turned out, I didn't come into the corral until the sun was starting down in the west. I found Hardin and his four gunmen playing poker in the shade of the barn. I went on into the corral and started to saddle up Mouse. Shade found me out there.

"No hard roping or herding for you today," he said. "Take the good horse. You might need a little more speed."

What, I wondered, did that mean? I saddled up Cisco and waited another thirty minutes while Hardin and his boys finished the poker game. By the time we hit the trail, I knew this was a night raid.

They set a steady pace moving north through Taylor land, but they weren't in a hurry, considering how fast that sun was setting. I was guessing we'd been out about three hours, and it was getting on to dusk when Hardin called a halt.

The path we'd followed was narrowing and about to disappear. I hadn't seen any Taylor cattle for a while. Hardin pulled us up on a low rise. I looked over the top and saw cattle grazing around a small pond below. Another quick glance told me there were no riders watching the cows. None that I could see, anyway. I wondered if they'd paid some cowboys to leave the herd.

Hardin lit a smoke and passed a bottle around. Once in a while, he seemed to check the sunset. I was sure he was waiting for the light to fade. When dusk set in, he sent the four gunhands down into the valley. They seemed to be looking for any hands that might still be guarding the cows, checking gullies and thickets of brush and trees.

Finally, they started gathering the herd. Shade rode over and pulled up beside me.

"You stay here," he said. "Watch for any strays

wandering off. Hardin will keep watch on the other side. When they have passed by, fall in behind. There will be two others behind you, watching." Then he rode down to help gather the herd and drive them out.

JW Hardin was across the hill from me, still smoking a cigar. It was too dark to see if he was watching me, but I'm betting he was.

The cows began to top the rise and stream past me. Hardin put out the cigar and took the lead. Shade and two gunhands were making a little more noise now, yipping at them and cracking a whip once in a while. When they had all passed me, I fell in behind. One glance behind me showed the other two hands using branches to cover over the trail. Good luck, I thought, covering the tracks of this many cows. Maybe they didn't care that much.

I held my spot behind the herd. The two behind me never passed me, but I'm sure they were back there somewhere. One or two cows tried to stray, but there was enough moon to see them, and I drove them back to the herd.

I said nothing all the way back. When we were close to the ranch, Shade rode up beside me again. "That's all we need from you, Nash," he mumbled. "The other boys and me will get them settled down in a pasture." He pressed something into my hand. It was five dollars.

He touched his spurs to his horse and rode away. I said nothing, but I had seen what I'm sure he didn't want me to see. There was just enough light as the first cows had gone past me. They were wearing the Lazy S brand. These were Sutton cows.

# Chapter 12
## *Drive to Austin*

I hung around the bunkhouse in the morning, hoping Curly would come and assign me some work. I would have even settled for more brush-poppin'. Anything but riding with Shade Taylor and JW Hardin to rustle more Sutton cattle would be fine with me. If they came looking for me, I had no idea how to get away and alert Murph back in Austin.

I left off looking over my shoulder for Shade Taylor when I saw the ranch owner, Creed Taylor, talking to somebody outside the corral. The guy looked familiar from what I could see of him, but he mostly had his back to me. Creed Taylor left off talking long enough to motion and holler for Curly to join them by the corral.

"We need an extra man to round up more stray cows that's still up north." I had been so busy watching Creed Taylor, Curly, and the other man that Shade Taylor caught me by surprise. I jumped a little when I heard that voice.

I swung around to look at Shade and was trying to

come up with a weak excuse when Creed Taylor barked my name.

"Walker!" I swung around to see Creed Taylor pointing at me and motioning for me to come over. The stranger turned to look, and I knew him! It was Charles Goodnight, nodding and saying something to Creed Taylor.

I glanced back over at Shade. He was plumb annoyed, that was easy to see, but there was nothin' at all he could do about it.

Shade dropped back and disappeared into the bunkhouse. I could hear him swearing under his breath. He might have said something about gathering up the cows later, but I wasn't paying any more attention to him.

Creed Taylor glanced back and forth between me and Charles Goodnight when I walked up. He looked curious, but he didn't ask me anything. He pointed at Goodnight, then jerked a thumb out toward the pasture.

"Goodnight, here, just bought two hunnerd cows offa me," Taylor boomed. "He's needin' a couple hands to help him drive the cows over to the railroad." He stared at me suspiciously. "Says he knows you, Walker. Wants you and Curly to drive 'em over. You leave now." With that, Taylor turned on his heel and headed for the ranch house.

"Ready?" Goodnight asked. "Because I'm ready to go just as soon as we have 'em rounded up. Houston and Texas Central Railroad in Austin. We load up there, and I'll take the herd on up to Fort Worth."

He glanced over at Curly. "Looks like you're

saddled and ready to go," he said. "I'll wait for Walker, here, to get his horse at the corral." He looked out at the pasture to the north. "Creed Taylor already has some boys out there to help. I'll take my pick from that bunch in the pasture."

Curly nodded and moved out. I looked at the bunkhouse. Shade Taylor and JW Hardin were on the steps, watching. They went back inside when Goodnight turned to look. Goodnight then waited outside the corral while I saddled Cisco, then fell in beside me when I moved toward the pasture.

"How's things?" he asked, looking back over his shoulder toward the bunkhouse. "Looks like you had some company just now." He leaned over the saddle to spit. "Murph thought you might need a little help out here." He grinned a little. "That singer, Victoria, she seemed a mite worried about you, too."

I pulled Cisco alongside Goodnight's horse and filled him in, as fast as I could, about how Shade Taylor and JW Hardin were rustling Sutton cattle. I didn't have a lot of time, as Curly was about to catch up to us, and we were getting close to the herd that Goodnight had bought.

"There's gonna be more rustling," I told him. "Shade Taylor said something about it to me right before the boss called me over." I thought about that for a second. "I don't know if Creed Taylor, the owner, knows about this or not."

Goodnight pulled up and waited while Curly rode toward us. "Maybe he doesn't wanna know much," he said thoughtfully. "As long as his herd keeps gettin' bigger, maybe he don't much care how it happens."

He waved Curly past us, and we followed to check out the herd Goodnight had bought. "I'll find a way to get you free for a while when we reach Austin," he promised. "I'll send you on some errands. You'll have a chance to get with Murch and decide what to do about the rustling."

* * *

Things were winding down with the show in Austin. It had been a great run here. The Texas crowds were hungry for the entertainment, and a lot more respectful than what Victoria had seen in gold-boom towns and cow camps.

There were going to be several weeks between the show's finish here in Austin and the engagement in Denver. Victoria had not yet agreed to make the trip to Denver. It would be a long ride, and she knew that. She had done her share of traveling in stagecoaches, and she didn't look forward to it. Three people across one of those stagecoach benches made for a tight fit. There had been some talk about a covered wagon, but they'd decided on stagecoaches. She'd been told they would follow the Goodnight-Loving Trail for the most part. They might even get an Army escort for part of the way.

There was a letter at the post office for her. A quick look told her it was from her mother—she would know that handwriting anywhere. She felt her stomach turn over as she opened it. A letter coming this soon after her visit could only be bad news. She pulled the letter from the envelope and started reading. The news wasn't terrible, but her mother seemed even more concerned than before about the ranch situation.

Victoria stopped outside the post office, holding the letter in both hands and wondering what she could do. On the one hand, her family might soon be involved in a range war they weren't prepared to fight. On the other, Nash may already be up to his eyeballs in a much bigger war between the Taylors and the Suttons.

She turned and walked back into the post office, dashing off a quick letter to her mother, telling her she would come out to the ranch in just about a week, after the show closed in Austin.

After posting the letter, she came out of the post office and turned south, moving along the street where she had found Murph the Ranger and Charles Goodnight several days before. She moved toward the café. Goodnight would have left to buy cattle by now, but maybe Murph would be here. Maybe, she thought, Murph was a creature of habit. Or maybe he just liked the food at this café.

Victoria's spirits rose when she spotted Murph at the same table where he had eaten before. Judging by the pile of food on his plate, he had just started breakfast, and it looked like he was eating alone. She crossed the room and stopped at Murph's table. He rose and pointed at an empty chair.

"Please, ma'am, take a seat," he urged her.

Victoria did as he suggested and asked for only coffee when a server scooted across the room to her.

Murph watched her as he chewed his latest mouthful, then washed it down with a slurp of coffee. He leaned his elbows on the table and looked at her knowingly. "You're wonderin' how your friend Nash is doing down there at the Taylor place," he guessed.

Victoria only nodded, her eyes never leaving his. Murph heaved a signed and leaned back. "Truth is, ma'am, I haven't got much of anything to report." He glanced at her sideways and kept going.

"As you know, Mr. Goodnight went down there to buy some cattle, and he was gonna look things over an' see what he could see of Nash. Well, he rode out a few days ago, but I haven't heard anything from him."

Victoria chewed her lip thoughtfully while she absorbed the news. She started to ask a question, then thought better of it. "Well, she said finally, where would you meet Charles Goodnight when he comes? Where could I find him when he comes to town?"

"Train station," Murph said without hesitation. "If he bought them cows, he'd likely ship 'em out of Austin by rail. He don't have any hands to drive 'em here by himself." Murph thought that over, then added a thought. "He'll have to borrow a coupla boys from Taylor to help him get the cows to Austin."

Murph took the last two bites of his breakfast, then set his fork down. He guessed her next question. "The train comes in from those parts around noon, one train every day," he told her. "You could check for cattle comin' in around that time."

Victoria nodded and rose, then sat down again. Murph raised one eyebrow and waited.

"It's about my family—my family ranch. It's the Ridley ranch. We're not a big operation. Just a few hundred head of cattle and a big garden. We...well, I don't suppose you've heard of us."

It was a statement, not a question, but Murph shook his head and waited for her to continue.

"We have about one thousand acres, and it's good land. Great source of water with a stream flowing through it." She hesitated. "I think it's the water that causing the trouble...trouble with the neighbors."

Murph took a notebook from his pocket and fished around in another pocket until he found a pencil. "What's the name of the neighboring spread?" he asked. "And what kind of trouble are you talking about? Shootin' trouble?"

Victoria shook her head. "No shooting. We think they might have poached a few head, and they like to try to scare my brother and father. We don't have a fence at the boundary. They seem to keep pushing their cattle closer to the water. Their name is Erskine, Rolling R brand," she finished.

Murph, head down, kept taking notes. "Where is your place, ma'am?" he asked. His pencil hovered over the paper, waiting for her answer.

"Victoria," she corrected him. "Please, just call me Victoria. Our ranch is a long day's ride from Austin. You hold south and east, just following the trails toward Houston. When you cross the Colorado River, you go another twenty miles. You'll see settlements here and there. Ask at any of them and they can direct you."

Murph said nothing while he finished taking notes. He looked up and leaned forward again. "We take this seriously, ma'am...Victoria. I don't have any men to send right now, but if they step up the poaching or start shootin', you just come or git somebody at your place to come out here to Austin. We'll surely come a-foggin' it."

Victoria smiled and reached across the table to

squeeze his hand. "Thank you, I feel better already," she said.

Murph rose when she stood to leave. She waved at him from the door and pushed out onto the street.

Murph sat down again, tapping the notes with the pencil point while he re-read what he had written. Then he folded up the notes and tucked them away in his pocket. He wouldn't forget. The Rangers were here to keep these things from getting worse. He really didn't have anyone to send right now, though.

He leaned back and waved for a coffee refill. He didn't have anyone to send now, but he did have an idea how to help the Ridley family. Murph glanced at the clock in the corner. That train should be coming in pretty soon.

\* \* \*

Victoria paused outside the café. Last night's performance had been the last in Austin. She owed a firm answer to the show's owners about whether she would go to Denver with them, and now she was nowhere close to an answer.

"Miss Victoria!"

The sudden call caught her by surprise. It wasn't a voice she recognized. Scanning the few people near her, her face lit up with recognition. It was Alec, the hand recently hired to help at the ranch. She moved to meet him.

Alec's hat was in his hand. "I been sent to bring you back to the ranch, ma'am," Alec mumbled. His hat passed from one hand back to the other. "There's...uh, doins' goin' on back there. Your ma, she wants you to come. I brung a horse for you."

Victoria's brain searched for an answer. "The last letter didn't say she was that worried," she blurted. "I've been checking at the post office every day."

Alec's hand went to his pocket. He brought out a crumpled piece of paper. Victoria smoothed it out, and she read the few lines quickly. She glanced toward the rail station with regret. There wasn't time.

"Let's go," she told Alec. "We can get my things at the hotel. I'll change clothes and be ready to ride in twenty minutes."

* * *

It took us two days to reach the railhead in Austin with Goodnight's cows. He said he didn't want 'em tuckered out before they got to the rail cars, so we took it pretty easy on them. Goodnight planned to ship them north to Fort Worth on the rails from here.

Goodnight had some tales about driving cows on the Goodnight-Loving Trail through to Denver and beyond while we herded the cows. It made me think that a drive should be in my plans. Curly just talked about finding a saloon when we got to Austin, so mostly it was just me and Goodnight talking about the drive.

We didn't talk anymore about the rustled cows at the Taylor place. I mostly trusted Curly, but we didn't really have any more to talk about. Goodnight told me he would help me get away for a few hours after we got to Austin, and that I could likely find Murph in the Sunrise Café, the same place where we'd met up before.

That's pretty much the ways things played out after

we delivered the cows to the railroad. Goodnight said he would stay to watch the critters getting loaded on the railcar. He handed me a letter and asked me if I would take it to his lawyer. Curly said nothing, just looking down the street at a saloon.

"Go on." Goodnight grinned. "You ain't talked about nuthin' else since we saddled up two days ago."

Curly grinned back, and we both led our horses to a livery stable just outside the railroad yard. "Meet you here in two hours?" he asked. Then he shaded his eyes and looked up at the sun. "Make it three," he decided.

I waved over my shoulder and proceeded down the street, looking for the address Goodnight had given me. When I finally found it, it turned out to be a bakery, not a law office. No matter, though—it was right next door to the Sunrise Café. I looked both directions and didn't see Curly. He was probably up to his eyeballs in beer already.

It was a hot day and that gave me ideas, so I ordered a pitcher of beer myself and waited to see if Murph would show up. Half an hour later, he did, and we started lowering the suds level in that pitcher. Murph took his time getting around to things.

He poured me the last glass of beer and looked around the room. "What've you got to tell me?" he blurted.

I didn't waste any time. I had plenty of time before I had to meet up with Curly, but I was hoping to pick up Victoria's trail here in town somewhere. I'd been thinking about finding her ever since we'd left the Taylor Ranch.

I looked back at Murph. "They're smugglin' Sutton cows," I told Murph abruptly. "They made me join 'em on one raid and there's another coming up. If the Suttons get wind of it, there's gonna be a shooting war. Taylor's got him some gunhands, too." I told him about Hardin, Shade Taylor and a few others.

Murph pulled a pencil and piece of paper from his pocket and shoved them across the table. "Draw the route, best you can," he said. "You think the second raid is just gonna be a little deeper into Sutton land, right?"

I nodded, then set to work, drawing in the Taylor ranch house and corrals first, and then I started to sketch in the path we'd taken on the first raid. It had been dark, but I thought I was pretty close with this map. Murph decided this was thirsty work and ordered us more beer.

Finally, I pushed the paper and pencil back across the table. I had a little X where I thought they would likely hit the Sutton herd. Murph studied it, nodded, and pushed the paper back into his pocket. He stood.

"Taylor's got men around here sometimes," he advised. "Might be best if you get on back. You think the raid is maybe as early as tomorrow night?"

I nodded.

"I'll have some boys there," he promised. "You just look sharp and get your noggin down outta the line of fire. Help us as best you can." He ducked out the door and disappeared.

I spent two hours looking around for Victoria at the theater, even though the play was closed, and at the hotel. Finally, I had to give up and went back to the livery stable. Curly was there and mounted up. His eyes were swimmin' around a little, but I decided he could make the ride.

* * *

Murph had a lot to do in a short while. First, he would have to round up at least two more Rangers, maybe three. He shook his head in frustration. There never seemed to be enough men for the job. He passed his hand over the paper in his pocket with the directions to the Ridley spread. He'd decided that Nash Walker couldn't be distracted just now. Murph would give him the paper later.

# Chapter 13
## *Going Home*

Victoria was now five miles down the road from Austin, on her way to the family ranch and riding next to Alec. No words had been spoken—he seemed willing to leave her alone with her thoughts until she was ready to talk.

Finally, Alec glanced at her sideways and cleared his throat slightly. "If there's anything you want to ask, Miss Victoria, I'll answer you just the best I can."

She nodded and frowned ahead at the trail. Where to start?

"Mom's letter just said things are getting worse. She said she knows the show has finished its run in Austin, and she asked me to come home with you. What did she mean when she said things have gotten worse? Has there been a shooting? Or a lot of cattle rustling? I can go back and get the Rangers if that's what happened."

Alec shook his head. "Nuthin' that big has been goin' on, but I think your pa has done been pushed to his limit. He's been fortin' up around there, and I think he's fixin' to stretch a fence across that upper pasture.

You know the property ain't that wide there at the top of the pasture. He's gonna run a fence across it."

Victoria slowed her horse and stared at Alec in surprise. "It's not that wide, but it would take days to build a fence across there. How's he expecting to get that done without the Erskine riders chopping it down as soon as he gets started?"

Alec let a slow grin cross his face. "Ever heard tell of sumthin' called barbed wire? Or Bobwire, or some kind of name like that."

Victoria shook her head.

"Yeah, me neither. It's wire, like it says, but it's got some nasty points stickin' out of it. Be really nasty to cut through. We figger we can stretch that across the upper pasture in a day. Specially if somebody was holding her rifle in the trees and watchin' out for us to keep them Erskine riders off our backs." He glanced sideways at that last sentence.

Victoria's jaw dropped open. "Is that why my mom wanted me to come home?"

Alec avoided her gaze. "That and just to help out. Your ma, she says you got more fight in you than the other three of you put together."

Victoria let a grin spread slowly across her face. "You give me that Henry rifle and I'll dust 'em off," she promised. They rode a short distance farther while some of the things Alec had told her started to sink in.

"Where did Dad get that barbed wire?" she asked. "Is it expensive?" Alec's shrug told her he didn't have the answer to those questions. "I'm surprised he's fighting back like this," she said.

Alec glanced over again. "Yore pa's an old campaigner," he murmured. "You've maybe not seen much of that, growin' up at the ranch and all, but he'll stand his ground. I'm proud to stand there with him. I expect he's been settin' some money aside to get ready." Alec chewed at his lower lip and waited before his next question to Victoria.

"That...uh, friend of yours, back there in Austin. I was hopin' maybe he would come out and stand with us. Nash something, I think. He looks salty to me. Got some bark on him. Do you think he'd come?"

Victoria shrugged, sighed, then shook her head. "I think he would if he knew about it and was able to come. He might be in a tighter spot than we are right now." She went on to explain about the Taylor-Sutton fight and how Nash might be in the middle of it. She didn't tell Alec that she had dropped off a note at Nash's old boardinghouse in Austin before leaving.

Alec said nothing. They rode until they crossed a small stream and stopped to water the horses.

"What else does Dad have planned?" she asked. "You said he's fortin' up. What does that mean besides the fence?"

Alec chuckled. "Yore pa has all kinds of surprises planned," he said. "We done dug us a couple rifle pits at the edge of the trees near the stream in the middle of the property. If'n they cut down that fence and get to the water, they'll get theirselves a hot welcome. Plus, he's cut a slot or two to slide a rifle through the doors at the ranch house. Your ma, she's been storing up water and food and such in the cellar."

Victoria whistled under her breath, then knelt at the stream alongside Alec to refill her canteen and grab a quick bite. Alec checked the overhead sun. "We'd best keep moving," he advised her. "We need to get to the ranch before dark. There's some country betwixt here and there that ain't real friendly."

*  *  *

I'd thought I might have to tie Curly into his saddle to get him back to the Taylor spread, but he hung in there better than I'd given him credit for. At first, I thought he was just one of those boys who could soak up his suds, but after a while, I started to wonder about some things.

I'm not naturally a suspicious man. Matter of fact, some folks would tell you I'm just too trusting. Other folks would tell you I trust 'em till I don't, and you don't wanna be around me too much after I learn not to trust you. I guess both things got some truth to 'em.

Either way, I was doin' okay with Curly bouncing along and belching ever' now and then, but he started asking questions about where I'd gone while he was at the saloon. What was Goodnight's lawyer like and stuff like that? I couldn't see much reason he would wonder about such things.

I told him almost nothing, and after a while, he stopped asking. Several miles down the road after that, he took to singing instead of asking questions. After about three miles of that awful caterwauling, I wished he'd go back to the questions. Was he just pretending to be drunk now?

The last hour, we picked up the pace. Nobody likes to ride the trails at night, and I don't think either one of us was sitting easy in the saddle, knowing some Taylor riders had rustled Sutton cows just a few nights ago. I heaved a little sigh after I'd turned Cisco into the corral.

Curly stripped off the saddle and lurched a little on

his way to the bunkhouse. I wasn't believing that lurch. He'd had hours to move on from whatever he'd tossed down his gullet at that saloon.

As I brushed Cisco, I kept the horse between me and bunkhouse and kept watch over Cisco's back. A light flickered on the bunkhouse porch when Curly got there, and I shot a glance at the bunkhouse. There were two people talking to Curly, then the torch moved away from the porch, and Curly went on into the bunkhouse, singing and gettin' himself cussed out by everybody inside there.

I couldn't be sure, but it might have been Shade Taylor and JW Hardin talking to Curly on that porch. He hadn't been their spy on this trip, had he? I didn't want to go from being too trusting to being too suspicious. There must be some solid ground in between. I just wasn't too sure I had found it.

I took my time doing things out there in the corral. I saw nothing of Shade Taylor or JW Hardin, and didn't see any of their gunhands, either. I thought they had four or five. You never saw all of 'em at one time or in one place.

I hid something in the barn when I'd finished with Cisco. I was pretty sure I would need it later. When there'd been no lights in the bunkhouse or the ranch house for at least a half hour, I eased out of the corral and found my cot in the bunkhouse. I was hoping I'd hear nothing else about *rounding up strays* from Shade Taylor or Hardin after tonight, but I wasn't holding my breath. I'd be watching Curly just as close as I watched those two from now on.

\* \* \*

Murph had wasted no time in putting together a squad to ride out to stop the feud between the Suttons and the Taylors. This was his worst fear—a range war. One of the Taylors had been shot a year ago. On top of that, Murph knew the Suttons must be aware that cattle had been poached. Bad Bob Sutton was too good a stock man not to notice that. Hardin and Shade Taylor were kidding themselves if they didn't think the Suttons were prepared for another round of it.

Murph didn't intend to sit in the middle of a shooting gallery when the Taylor gunmen came back to the Sutton pastures. He was sitting with three other officers on a rise overlooking the Sutton ranch house, watching while four horsemen came toward them. Murph had no doubt the one in front was Bad Bob Sutton himself, the former Ranger.

Murph had never served with Sutton, but that's why he had Abel Harmon with him. Harmon knew Sutton had worked with him, and Murph hoped they could talk. It was the only way to stop a shooting war. Or Murph corrected himself, maybe they could prevent it long enough for him to think of a way around it later on.

When the Sutton hands came within fifty yards, Harmon walked his horse slowly to meet them. He reined in and took off his hat, letting Bob Sutton see and recognize him. Sutton moved forward, leaving the other three where they were. Murph watched while the two men talked. Sutton waved his arms a few times, but Harmon stayed calm, letting him talk.

Finally, Sutton turned and rode back toward his house. His men trailed after him. Harmon turned and waved the Rangers forward. Murph smiled grimly. At least Sutton was willing to talk. That was something, anyway.

Five minutes later, Murph and Harmon were seated on the porch of Sutton's ranch house. The two other Rangers and two of Sutton's men were scattered around the railing of the porch. Everybody was armed.

Murph glanced around, then concentrated on Sutton. "There's a lot of folks on this porch," Murph drawled lazily. "How about if my two men go back out with the horses and your two boys stand down, too? We're just here to talk."

Sutton stared without blinking, then glanced sideways at Harmon. "Kin I trust him?" he growled.

Harmon nodded slowly. Sutton waved at his two men standing at the railing and muttered something. Murph waved off his two men as well. The Rangers moved out to stand with the horses in the yard. Murph exhaled slowly. It was a start.

"They rustled some cows," Sutton barked, staring at Murph across the porch.

No use denying it, Murph thought. "I know they did," he agreed. "And I've heard they're plannin' another raid. I brought my boys to stop it. We're gonna get your cows back that they took already. Give me a chance to do it without a shootin' war, that's what I'm asking."

Long moments dragged by. Sutton reached into his pocket, pulled out a cigar, and took his time lighting it. "How you gonna do all this?" he asked.

Murph looked at Harmon, then reached into his pocket and took out the map drawn for him by Nash Walker. "They're gonna strike right here," he said, pointing at the map. "We'll be waitin' for them. They can come with us peaceful or not, but they're not gettin' any cows. Then we're gonna pay a visit to the Taylor ranch with as many men as I need. We'll be watchin' for your brand when I check that stock."

Sutton stared at the map and blew two smoke rings. He watched Murph narrowly through the smoke. "I'm gonna be there when you're waitin' for 'em," he announced.

Murph shook his head. "You gotta let us do this by ourselves," he insisted.

Five minutes later, Sutton hadn't budged. "I'm there or I'll be there with my boys and turn 'em loose on them Taylor riders," he growled. "You and your boys can be in my way or not if I do that. Them's my terms."

Murph heaved a deep breath. "You don't shoot," he warned Sutton. "You watch."

Sutton shrugged. "If they shoot at me, I'm shootin' back," he growled. "I got the right to do that."

Murph glanced at Harmon and decided to take Sutton's terms. It was the best he was likely to get. They agreed to meet at the spot on Nash Walker's map for each of the next two nights. Murph joined his men and rode away, followed by Sutton, heading for the place where they would wait for Taylor's men. It was the best chance he had to stop a shooting war.

Or, he corrected himself, maybe he could at least postpone a shooting war while he kept working on this. Sometimes, he told himself, you just have to take what you can get and keep trying.

* * *

The first day back was quiet. Too quiet to suit me. Curly put me out to do some fence repair, and I was out there by myself. That suited me just fine. I didn't know who to trust, so Cisco was as much company as I needed.

Come dinnertime, the only one that came over to talk to me was Creed Taylor, the owner of the joint. Curly had parked himself on the bench next to me for just a minute to ask about fence repairs, then he cleared out when Creed Taylor sat down.

"Did ya get them cows delivered to the railroad okay?" he asked.

"Yup. Sure did." I stuffed a big bite of steak in my mouth and commenced chewing. I didn't want to talk any more than I had to.

Creed Taylor nodded and said, "Good customer, that Goodnight is. Got to keep the good ones happy." He took a bite and stared at the ranch house for a minute. "He said he might have some errands for you to run in town. You and Curly get that done for him?"

I didn't know what Curly had told him, so I decided to tell him the truth. "I run some papers over to his lawyer's office," I said. "Curly had him a powerful thirst by the time we got to town."

He laughed about that and seemed to relax. When he got up and left, I'd told him the truth, but I'd left out one thing. I had picked up my new Winchester 73 in Austin. Working out there by myself on the fences today, I'd gotten it sighted in and was mighty pleased with it. If Hardin and Shade had me on any more raids, I would have that rifle wrapped in a blanket, and I would take it with me.

\* \* \*

My luck didn't hold the next morning. I was the first one in the chow line at breakfast, and I'd already decided just to send myself back out to mend fences. I bolted down my bacon and biscuits, guzzled a little coffee and was hot-footing it out to the corral when I heard Shade Taylor's voice.

"Kinda in a hurry ain't ya?"

I shrugged. "Daylight's burnin'. I've got a few places to patch on the fences Curly had me workin' on yesterday. Done by lunchtime, I figger."

Shade nodded like he was listening, which he wasn't. His eyes traveled down to my waist, lingered for a minute on my Colt, then he said what I didn't wanna hear. "We're gonna round up a few more cows tonight. Probly the last bunch we'll have to get. Be back here before dinner. We'll ride out then."

He didn't wait to hear an answer from me, just turned on his heel and walked away. I went out to the barn, retrieved my Winchester from where I hid it yesterday, and slid it into the scabbard. I checked the Colt and the Winchester for ammo, then headed out to the fences. I was as ready as I could get.

It was mid-afternoon and maybe a little later when I came in, judging by the sun overhead. I'd have put it closer to four than to three. I went looking for Cookie and begged for some early supper from him. I had a feeling we'd be gone by chowtime. There was maybe an hour of daylight left when Hardin and Shade Taylor formed up the crew and rode out.

All of the gunhands were on this trip, plus Hardin and Shade Taylor. When we strung out a little on the trail, they seemed to herd me to the middle of the pack. I wasn't liking my odds.

Darkness fell with only a quarter moon to guide us. Hardin was leading the way along with two of the gunslingers. Shade Taylor and the other gunhand were behind me. Nobody was talking. The creak of saddle leather was about the only thing I could hear.

We passed the valley where we'd rustled the cows the other night and kept pushing on to the north. We crossed a low ridge, and Hardin had enough sense to hold low and move along the side of it, not skylining us. I wondered if he had any idea he could be walking into a squad of Texas Rangers.

Shade moved up beside me. "You and me will go down and get the cows this time," he said.

I waited for a while to answer. "Are they Taylor cows?" I finally asked.

He gave a long, cold look. "What if they ain't?" he snarled.

"Then I ain't getting 'em".

Shade Taylor cursed and moved to join Hardin. I could hear them talking for a while before Hardin dropped back behind me.

We came down from the ridge and moved toward another valley. Hardin was slowing the pace now, and I sensed Shade and the other gunhand closing the gap behind me. When Hardin held up a hand to stop, he moved to the side a little. That was my cue.

I turned Cisco about one quarter to the side as my hand swept down for my Colt. Shade had moved out of the way to let his gunhand shoot me from behind. I saw the flame stab from his gun, but I'd already fired. Even in that dim light, I saw him drop from the saddle.

Shade Taylor drew and fired just as I grabbed my Winchester and dove from the saddle. I felt a blow low on my right side as I turned and fired at Shade. He cursed, grabbed his arm and laid low over the saddle, moving sideways.

I crawled into some brush and worked my way in deep. I brought up the Winchester and waited, feeling the pain sweep over me. I wondered if I could stay awake long enough to keep the Taylor riders off me.

# Chapter 14
## *Trapped*

There was a lot of confusion out there. That was the only thing I felt sure of. One of the Taylor gunhands was down and probably dead. I'd seen my shot knock him off his saddle, and I knew where I had put that shot. He'd been quiet since I had burrowed into this thicket, and I could barely see the body lying where it had fallen. I had probably just grazed Shade Taylor, but he might have lost his appetite for coming after me. Once in a while, I'd hear him cuss over there, which was stupid, but I was saving my shots for when I could do more damage.

I reached down and touched my side. It was wet. I couldn't really see, but I knew it was blood. I could smell it. A fresh wave of nausea passed over me. I cut off a sleeve from my shirt and used it to tie my bandana over the wound. If I was lucky, the bullet had passed through without hitting anything vital. Right now, I just knew it hurt. I fought the urge to retch into the bushes.

Hoofbeats approached from down the trail. That could only be JW Hardin and the other two gunhands coming back to see how things had turned out. I'd been expecting them, and I was ready, if I could stay alert enough. I could hear Hardin calling out in a low voice. Shade Taylor answered. I couldn't get a fix on his position enough to get off a good shot.

It dawned on me I had nothing but enemies out there. I might as well discourage 'em from looking for me. Four against one didn't sound like good odds, and that's what I was working with. I moaned a little as I eased up onto my elbows and worked the Winchester's lever to fire three searching shots toward the voices out there.

They got quiet after that, and I didn't know if that was good or bad. Most likely, they had spread out and were trying to sneak up on me. They had some idea where I was after those three shots. I was pretty sure they couldn't see through the thick brush around me, but they could home in on the noise.

I passed an arm across my forehead to mop the sweat away. It was a cool night, but I seemed to be sweating and shivering at the same time. I adjusted my position a little and heard another little moan escape me. I needed some water, but the canteen was on my saddle, and I didn't know where Cisco had gone.

More hoofbeats were coming this way now. I hoped it was Murph and the Rangers. Maybe they'd been close enough to hear the shots. There was some yelling, then at least a half dozen shots, then more hoofbeats. I didn't know what to make of it. The sounds died away, and I fought to keep my eyes open.

Somewhere along the way, I must have passed out. I didn't know anything else until the gray light of dawn filtered through the bushes. I was surprised to find out I was still alive.

* * *

Murph had his three Rangers spread out along the tree line at the edge of a meadow. Sutton cattle grazed peacefully below. Bad Bob Sutton said he had about fifty head down there. It was enough to make a target for rustlers, but it was a small enough target they could hit and run.

Sutton had followed along quietly enough, but Murph didn't trust Sutton to stay quiet if a raid happened. He had Sutton several yards behind the Rangers. Sutton's rifle was still in the scabbard—Murph had made sure of that. That didn't mean it would stay in the scabbard if the rustlers came, though.

The horses stamped their hooves and swished their tails occasionally, but that was the only noise Murph could hear besides the cattle moving quietly while they grazed down below. A thousand questions and doubts ran through Murph's mind. This was the second night they had kept watch here. Nothing had happened last night. Darkness had fallen a couple hours ago, and Murph would have expected them before now if they were coming.

He had dismounted to give his horse a little water when three shots rang out. Murph's head snapped up, and he stared south, past the valley they'd been watching. He raced around to remount and pulled his pistol as he leaped into the saddle.

"Form a skirmish line!" he shouted, moving them down into and through the valley. The cattle milled and began to run past them, away from the gunfire. The Rangers maintained their positions as best they could, then reassembled a skirmish line as they climbed out of the valley.

More gunfire erupted before they crested the valley. Murph could feel and hear the concentration of fire coming from his left. "Watch left!" he shouted. "Return fire only! We have a man in there!"

A volley of fire came at them, and a Ranger fell from his saddle. The others dismounted and knelt to present a smaller target as they returned fire. Murph dismounted to check his man on the ground. Sutton rode past them, firing into the group of rustlers on his left. The Rangers held their fire as Sutton rode into the fight. The gunfire quieted, then died away as Sutton pursued them into the night.

"Hold your fire and hold your ground!" Murph shouted. "Form around me!" The Rangers reformed in a circle, guns up and ready. Murph knelt over the wounded man. The night fell strangely quiet as the sound of retreating hoofbeats died away.

"We've got to get this man back in the saddle and get him to a doctor!" Murph called in a low voice. A quick check told him the man had taken the shot low in his chest. He didn't seem able to move. After getting the wounded man in the saddle and assigning one of the two remaining Rangers to ride beside him and hold him in, Murph knew there wasn't much chance of finding Nash Walker in the dark.

After a quick circle of the area, they found a dead man the Taylor riders had left behind. Murph decided to return and give the man a burial the next day. He would search for Nash Walker then. He led the

Rangers on the trail back to Austin, knowing his wounded man was unlikely to survive.

* * *

My eyes fluttered open when I heard a bird singing somewhere near me. My side throbbed, and my mouth was bone dry. I pushed myself to a sitting position and peered through the surrounding brush.

There was somebody down and not moving, lying at the side of a narrow trail about twenty yards away from me. I was pretty sure that was the Taylor gunhand I had shot. I frowned and thought, trying to remember if it was only last night they had come after me. I decided it was.

I had my new Winchester and Colt, and not much else. Any water, food, and ammunition I had was on Cisco, and he was nowhere to be seen. I used the Winchester to push myself to a standing position. There were a lot of tracks out there, but nothing else.

Water was the first thing, I decided. There had been cattle out there not far from here, at least according to Shade Taylor and JW Hardin. If there were cattle, they had to be getting water from somewhere nearby.

I unloaded the Winchester and used it for a crutch, setting my course along the narrow trail I'd seen. That was the direction Hardin and his gunslingers had taken last night. I expected I would find cows grazing before I went much farther.

I wound along the trail between some oak trees and came out at the edge of a small meadow, forming a bowl just below me. A mixed herd of cattle was grazing.

I worked my way slowly down into the valley, leaning on the Winchester and keeping an eye out for any bulls that might want to challenge me. I was in no shape for that. They kept on grazing, stopping to stare at me once in a while.

I looked down at myself and can't say I blamed them for staring. There was dried blood on my lower right side. One sleeve was gone and my hat was back there somewhere. My pants were torn from crawling into the brush. I wasn't ready to undo my homemade bandage and take a look at the wound. I just needed water.

Coming uphill on the other side of the meadow was a lot tougher than coming down, but I took my time. Stopping for a breather at the top, I waited for a while before I set sail again. There didn't seem to be a trail on this side, but after a while, I could see a small game trail of some kind winding into a stand of post oak trees. That was a good sign. Maybe the deer had followed this path to water.

About two minutes later, I could see the shimmer of a small pond of water. Even better, it wasn't long before I could hear the gurgle of water. That had to be a creek feeding the pond. I could drink from that creek.

There was something else I could see as I emerged from the trees, and it was the most welcome sight of all. My horse Cisco was drinking at the edge of the pond. He came when I clucked at him. There was a rope on the saddle, so I used that to tether him to a tree limb at the water's edge.

Right after that, I was kneeling down by the creek, sipping slowly at first, pausing to look around, then drinking until I'd had enough. The canteen on my saddle was full, and I rooted around in the saddlebag until I came out with a little jerky and a biscuit.

Finally, I sat down by the creek and unwound the sleeve and bandana covering the wound on my side. It was ugly, but there was no fresh blood, which I took to be a good sign. The medics in the Army always said to keep open wounds covered. I didn't have anything else to use for a bandage, so I washed out the same bandana in the creek as best I could and bandaged up the wound again.

With a final check on Cisco, I realized I was struggling to stay awake. Sleep, I figured, might be the best thing. I found a small hollow area next to a fallen log, unsaddled Cisco, and dragged the saddle over to use for a pillow. Sleep came to me in a hurry.

\* \* \*

Murph was in a foul mood when he arrived at the scene of last night's dust-up. The wounded Ranger, one of his new men, had died during the all-night ride back to find a doctor in Austin. Murph's first chore this morning this morning had been to deliver the Ranger to the undertaker for burial and to write a letter to his family. His second chore after arriving on the scene was to bury the Taylor Ranch gunslinger.

Murph took off his jacket and pulled a shovel from his saddle. He had just one man with him today, but they both bent to the task, and an hour later, they had buried the unknown gunman. Bob Sutton showed up just as they finished. He had pursued the remaining gunmen last night—Sutton said there were four of them, but all had gotten away.

At least, Murph reflected grimly, he'd had an answer when Sutton had angrily demanded a return of the rustled cows taken several nights ago. Captain Leander McNelly had left with a squad of his men to visit the Taylor Ranch and to settle the issue.

Murph had a pretty good idea how that would go. McNelly would announce that Taylor had twenty-four hours to help return some *missing stock* from the Sutton Ranch. If that failed to happen, Taylor would be subject to a thorough check of all livestock. Rustlers would be hanged on the spot.

Sutton, calming down after Murph's news, agreed to help search for Nash Walker. Murph had brought his best tracker, but it turned out that Sutton was a better tracker than either of them. There was a fresh set of tracks leading out of some brush and moving to a trail leading to the meadow where Murph and the Rangers had laid in wait for the rustlers.

Sutton kneeled beside the tracks where they joined the trail. He pointed at an oval-shaped impression beside the tracks. "He's using his rifle butt to prop himself up," Sutton observed. "We got us an injured man." He stood to follow the tracks, but Murph held up a hand and went back to inspect the circle of brush where the tracks had started.

"Yep, he's injured," Murph called out. "There's a lot of pretty fresh blood in here." He stood and stared down the trail. "We gotta move careful," he advised. "He might be laid up in some more brush out there, and he might just have hisself an itchy trigger finger. We identify ourselves as we go."

Feeling certain the rustlers had all cleared out of the area, they proceeded along the trail, across the meadow, and up into a stand of post oak trees. Murph stopped every fifty yards to call out, "Walker!" There had been no answer so far.

Fanning out from the trees on the other side of the oak trees, they came to a small pond. Several cows were drinking at the pond. Sutton held up a hand and pointed to the other side of the water, where a bay horse stood tethered to a tree limb.

"Everybody hunker down," Murph ordered. Kneeling near the trunk of a large oak tree, Murph made a trumpet of his hands. "Walker!" he barked. "Nash Walker! It's Murph!"

\* \* \*

For the second time on the same day, I came to in a pile of brush with my head swimming and my side hurting. I tried to focus. There seemed to be a squirrel right overhead, scolding me and dancing along the limb of a post oak.

When I heard my name, I snapped up, then grabbed my side and moaned. I lay still for a moment, collecting myself and trying to make sense of hearing my name yelled out here in the middle of nowhere. I didn't recognize the voice so much, but when Murph announced himself, I climbed slowly out of the brush.

Three men came toward me slowly. They were staring just about as much as the cows in the meadow had stared this morning. I didn't have to look at myself this time to wonder why. I took a couple steps, and Murph waved his hands in the air. "We're comin' to you," he barked. "Stay there."

Murph I knew, and I recognized Bob Sutton from

the time he'd braced me on the trail. I didn't know the third guy, but the badge he wore told me enough. I stayed where I was and watched them come in.

"Murph," I said, "I never thought you was exactly a handsome man, but I gotta say you look pretty good to me right now."

The other two chortled, and Murph just shook his head. "Save your breath," he said. "We'll get you loaded up on your hoss and get you to a doc in Austin. You kin tell me what happened later. I got a pretty good idea, anyway."

That suited me fine. I wasn't feeling chatty right then. The ride wasn't a Sunday picnic, but they got me to a doc in Austin. He clucked over me a few times, poked and prodded, then finally let me go to sleep. I needed that.

* * *

Victoria was feeling a little more relaxed as she rode up to the ranch house with Alec. The trip had gone quickly and they hadn't seen any riders or any sign of trouble on the way in. Alec had told her Carl Erskine, the neighbor, had maybe three or four gunhands on the payroll now. They'd seen no sign of them.

Her mother rushed out the door to give her a hug, followed by her father and her brother. Alec took the horses to the corral while Victoria joined the family for dinner. It wasn't until after they had eaten and the dishes were cleared from the table that her father started to talk about the ranch and the neighbor.

"They've been rustlin', just a cow or two at a time," he told her. "Maybe they just wanna aggravate me or

maybe they want a shootin' war they think I can't win."
He stopped and watched Victoria from across the table.

"Alec told you I've got some of that bob-wire?" he
asked.

Victoria nodded. "Yes, I've heard of barbed wire.
You have enough to cover the property line at the top of
the upper pasture?"

"Yup." Her father's jaw was set in a grim line.
"We've done dug the post holes and got 'em ready to go,
too." He nodded at her brother Rusty. "Well, he
allowed, we've got all but two of 'em dug. I've set ever'
fifteen feet along that ridge. We'll dig two more come
first light, set the poles and string that wire before they
know what hit 'em."

"Tonight?" Victoria's jaw dropped. "In the morning,
I mean? You're going to have the wire strung that soon?"

He nodded, watching her closely. "We've got Alex
back now, and we're countin' on you to watch our backs
with your Henry while we string it. You in?"

"Yes," she answered quickly. She glanced over at
her mother, who was staring at the table. She looked
back at her father. "I'll do it." She would talk to her
mother about this later.

* * *

A talk with her mother later that night had confirmed
what she'd thought—her mother was against it. It was
too late to do anything else about that now, she thought.
Her father was determined to fight back, and she agreed
with him.

Now, with a light mist falling and the early dawn
getting brighter, she lay at the top on the ridge at the

edge of the tree line, watching for any sign of movement. Her father, Rusty, and Alec had made short work of digging the last two holes and dropping the posts in. They were firmly in place now and would be hard to pull up.

Stretching and hammering the wire had taken probably less than an hour. When the three of them finished that and joined her at the tree line, she had still seen no movement out there. They moved out and mounted up to go home for breakfast.

Somehow, the morning quiet left her a little unsettled. Could they have been watching all along and she just didn't know? Was this how range wars got started?

# Chapter 15
## *Erskine's Gamble*

Carl Erskine was in a tighter spot than anybody else knew. His wife had left him six months before, distraught over the hiring of gunfighters instead of ranch hands. He'd told the story to anybody that would listen that she had gone to visit family in California, but folks were starting to suspect she wasn't coming back. That wouldn't have been such a problem, but ranch hands and gun hands tended to stick around when they got good food. Even Erskine couldn't kid himself, the food wasn't good anymore.

That wouldn't have been so bad, but four of his five hands were mostly gunhands. There was only one cattleman in the bunch, and Erskine was a little worried that Duffy, his cattleman, had long since figured out that Erskine couldn't support this many cows with the water they had on the property. The Rolling R needed cowboys, and Erskine couldn't pay them.

On top of that, the bank was starting to demand payments on the land and the house. Erskine didn't have the money without selling off all his cows. He was months away from losing his ranch to the bank.

Erskine heaved a sigh and moved out to take a seat on the front porch swing. All of this brought him back to the ranch water problem. He'd been watering some stock at night at the stream on his neighbor Ridley's property, but now that confounded barbed wire fence was stretched across the property border, blocking his way.

That left an all-out attack on Ridley and his family as his only solution. There was no other way he could see to do this. Erskine would be an outlaw if he attacked his neighbor and word got around. He didn't really want to be an outlaw, but there was no way he was going back to working in a factory in Pennsylvania. He'd come here fifteen years ago with a young wife, high hopes, and a little inherited money. This ranch was all he had left.

Erskine watched as his cook came out to ring the triangle for breakfast. Erskine could barely call this guy a cook, but that's all he had. Evans, the guy who called himself the cook, had been injured on a cattle drive to Kansas several years back. He could barely get around on his one good leg. He'd helped the cook a little on his last cattle drive. Now he claimed to be a cook himself. Erskine gave him nothing other than a spot to sleep in the barn and free food. It's all he could afford. Evans could fry bacon and cook beans. That was it. All the hands had sworn off his biscuits after one try. Erskine's stomach knotted up just thinking about the coffee.

After breakfast, Erskine excused Duffy to check on the cattle and sent Evans back to the kitchen. The other four hands stayed on the porch, watching him warily.

Erskine was pretty sure they had rustled a few head of Ridley's stock and sold them during these last several weeks. He really didn't mind if they did that. If they made some extra money, he didn't have to pay them as much. Unfortunately, the fence had put a stop to that.

A redhead who called himself Hawk fancied himself to be the leader of this bunch. Erskine kept his eyes on Hawk while he talked. Hawk crossed his arms and slouched against the railing.

"We gotta have more water," Erskine said bluntly. "I guess all you boys know that." They all nodded. "We gotta get the water from that stream south of us. That means we gotta cut that wire and go in. Might as well take his cows while we're there."

They stared at each other uneasily. Erskine felt a flush of anger climbing up from his neck to his face. "There's four of you," he pointed out. "How many guns they got over there?"

"Two," Hawk answered quickly. "Unless you count the boy. They've got old man Ridley and a hand they call Alec. He might be a little better with the rifle than Ridley." He fell silent and looked at the other three.

"What?" Erskine demanded angrily.

"What about the woman?" Hawk asked. "Ridley's wife? Plus, we've seen another woman there, time to time. Mebbe his daughter. What do you expect us to do with the women? Ain't gonna be no safe place for us in Texas or nowhere else if we hurt the women."

Erskine felt the anger boil away. He stared at Hawk, then shifted his gaze out to the pasture behind the ranch house. He hadn't thought about the women. Erskine stood and started for the back door of the house. "Let me worry about the women," he growled. "You take care of the fence and them cows. Shoot first if you want to. Don't need to ask no questions."

Hawk stopped him with one more thing just as Erskine opened the door. "We got some squatters livin' in the line cabin on the far north end of the ranch. They might be a pretty salty bunch. You know about them?"

Erskine turned around. This was something else he didn't know. "How long?" he asked. "How many?"

Hawk shrugged. "I'd say three men hiding out up there. Two days, maybe less. I just seen 'em yesterday."

Erskine stared at his boots. "You let me worry about them, too," he mumbled. Then he disappeared inside.

* * *

The ride to get here with his two remaining gunhands had been long and a little painful for Shade Taylor. He'd left one man dead on the ground, JW Hardin had deserted them the first chance he got, and Taylor himself had a painful graze across his arm from a shot by Nash Walker.

That he'd found this cabin was partly because of good memory and partly because of luck. He'd hidden out this way before, but it had been at least five years ago, and he'd been trying to find it in the dark when they came here two nights before. Shade had been happier than he'd let on when the dawn light yesterday morning had revealed this cabin, nestled in a ravine at the far edge of somebody's pasture, with a trickle of water from a stream running by outside the cabin.

Shade peeled back the bandage around his upper arm and inspected the deep graze running at an angle across his arm. He grimaced and wrapped a new bandage around it, holding one end of the rag in his teeth to tie the knot. He glared at the two other men in the cabin, who clearly weren't going to lift a hand to help.

Shade muttered darkly while he finished with the bandage. He owed Nash Walker double for this situation. One, for turning tables on them the other night, leaving Shade with this wound plus a dead gunhand. Two, those men had come up out of the grazing meadow in formation when they attacked the Taylor raiders. They had either been from the Army or else they were Texas Rangers. Shade reserved a special hatred for anybody who brought in the law.

One of the men in the room with him now was named Eli. Shade had ridden with Eli for a number of years and trusted him. The other man was expendable. Shade called him Rex because he reminded Shade of a dog he'd had as a kid. The dog was mostly loyal, but you still had to keep an eye on him so you didn't get bit. As long as this guy he called Rex answered to that name, Shade didn't care about the real name. He trusted Rex about as much as he'd trusted that dog.

Eli stood and stared out the one window of the cabin. He tensed, then announced over his shoulder, "Rider coming." He kept watching as Shade stood and moved toward the window. "He's wavin' a flag," Eli added. "A white flag."

Shade moved up to join Eli at the window. He snorted mirthlessly. "He ain't even got here yet and he's surrenderin'," Shade told the others. "I reckon we can stay in this here cabin as long as we want. Let's go hear what he's got to say."

Their visitor reined in his horse about twenty yards

from the cabin and watched as Shade and Eli approached on foot. His glance flicked back and forth from the two of them to the cabin behind them.

This guy known, Shade reflected, that there was somebody in the cabin already when he rode out here. Why else would he approach with a white flag? The man's glances back and forth at the cabin told Shade this guy at least suspected a third man holding a gun on him from the cabin. Shade kept those thoughts in mind while he stopped and waited for the visitor to speak.

The man stayed on his horse, then lowered his white flag carefully and stowed it away in his saddle. "Welcome, boys," he told them. "I own this here ranch, and I might have a way for you to make some money, if you're interested."

Thirty minutes later, with all four of them seated on some logs thrown down outside the line cabin, Erskine had introduced himself and made his pitch. Shade Taylor noticed that the man didn't seem to care who they were. He hadn't bothered to learn anything about them.

The deal he offered was in exchange for helping him drive out a neighbor and also helping him steal the man's cattle. Shade and his two hands would receive half the profit from the neighbor's herd. But the man had cautioned he would only need their help if his present plan failed. He would like them to stick around until he found out about that.

Shade could see all kinds of problems with the proposal, but he was already thinking about getting a lot more than the man was offering. The guy's present plan probably involved having other gunmen driving out the neighbor. Erskine must not have much confidence in the gunmen he had now, or this conversation would have never happened. Plus, there was probably more to it than just driving an old man off his ranch.

Still, this had possibilities. They could use this cabin until the man found out if his hands could take care of this. If they couldn't, those guys might still kill off some of the shooters at the neighbor's ranch and lower the odds. There were probably women or a family involved, but that didn't bother Shade. He could make them go away.

The price, though, would be a lot more than half the cattle. It would be the neighbor's ranch and all the cattle, with water rights given to Erskine for his cows. It would at least be that, Shade corrected himself. He might just take both ranches.

Shade reached out to shake the man's hand. "We have a deal," he agreed. "We'll wait to hear from you." He stood and thought of one more thing. "We'll need one of your cows," he said. "We ain't had much food up here."

"I'll have my man bring one up." Erskine raised a hand to tip his hat, then rode away.

Shade Taylor waited for Erskine to ride out of view, then turned to his men. "Rex!" he growled, "make yourself useful. Track him back to his place. See what it looks like, find out what you can about the neighbor's place. See if any shootin' gets started, then hightail it back here and tell me what you know."

\* \* \*

I had been stretched out on a cot in the back room of a doc's office for two days now. Doc was a grumpy old guy with a big pile of white hair on his head. He didn't seem to like me very much. I guess that made us even. He came in once a day to make me miserable. At least they brought me three squares a day and the doc let me sit in a chair out on the porch for a couple of hours twice a day.

I saw Doc Abrams coming for me now and gave him the old fisheye. He ignored me and unwrapped the wound, then got down and stared at it and mumbled a few things. He poked me a few times, then stood back and grunted with satisfaction.

"I'm gonna let you go tomorrow," he announced. I smiled at him for the first time.

He looked at me and asked, "You don't like me much, do you?"

"Not just you," I said. "I ain't been likin' docs much since I was a kid. My ma, she had a doc back in Tennessee, and I had to pay him off with moonshine. Ma would give him more than he had comin' anyway, and then if I was laid up, he took an extra jug from the still on his way out."

Doc looked at me for a long time, then laughed and waved his hand. "Murph says he'll come later. You can tell him I'll let you go tomorrow." He walked away, and I heard him mumbling something about getting paid in moonshine. It sounded to me like he was in favor of it.

Murph had a surprise for me when he visited the next day. He had stopped by the boardinghouse where I'd stayed before when I was in Austin. He said he had a note for me. I took one look and knew from the handwriting that it was from Victoria.

Murph waited while I unfolded the note and read

it. I stuck it in my pocket and started up from my chair. Murph put out a hand to stop me.

"She's gone to her family's ranch," I said. "There might be some trouble brewing and I'm gonna get out there."

"Do you know where you're going?" Murph asked.

Well, sir, that stopped me. I surely didn't know. I looked at Murph. "Do you?"

"I do." Murph nodded. "But I ain't ready to go today. Maybe tomorrow after I talk to the doc. Things have settled down for a while with the Taylors and Suttons, though I don't expect it will last. I won't let you get in the middle of anything when you're just mending, unless I come along to keep an eye on you."

"Doc says I can go," I called out. I left out the part about him not letting me go until tomorrow.

He moved toward the door of the doctor's office. "You go on back to the boardinghouse for tonight. I'll check in with you tomorrow."

\* \* \*

The attack still hadn't come, two days after the barbed wire had been strung, but Victoria found little comfort in that. The constant watchfulness would wear them all down, eventually. Her father had stayed up the first night, watching for anyone trying to cut the wire. Nothing had happened, and they didn't have the manpower to keep up a nightly watch.

This morning, in the early morning light, she had ridden to the top of the pasture with her father and Alec. There'd been no visible cutting on the wire, but even in the dim light, they were reluctant to show themselves as any kind of target at the top of the ridge. They didn't dare ride along the fence line to inspect more closely.

Victoria had brought binoculars she'd been given by a customer at one of her shows. When the light strengthened as the sun rose, she studied the wire from the cover of the trees fifty yards down the slope. She still couldn't see any cuts in the wire.

Now, back at the house and sitting at the breakfast table with her mother, she voiced some doubts while her mother served coffee and biscuits.

"I don't know if we can stop anybody if they cut through the wire," she observed gloomily. "We don't know how many men they have. We could retreat to the rifle pit by the stream if we see them coming, but we could be overrun and cut off from the house out there."

Her mother said little, and Victoria realized she was only raising issues her mother was already worried about. She had no answers to Victoria's concerns, and she was looking more worried by the minute.

Victoria bit her lip and resolved not to discuss it with Margie, her mother, again. They went to inspect the food reserves available in the house. Along with a good stockpile of food, there was a supply of bandages, scissors, and as many emergency supplies as they thought they would need.

She left her mother sorting through the food supplies and went to the front room, where the rifles and ammunition were stored. It was a grim reminder of the situation they were in. Running to the barn for more bullets might not be a choice if the attack came.

Her father, Matt Ridley, came through the front door just as she finished making a count of the boxes of ammo. He motioned at her. "Ride with us," he said. "Alec and I are going to take some cows up to the stream for water. We'll make sure everything is still okay."

Alec joined Matt outside the corral and waited while Victoria saddled her mare. She wrapped the leather strap of the binoculars around the saddle horn and slid her Henry rifle into the scabbard before they rode out.

They had broken the cattle into several groups and kept them closer to the house than usual to discourage rustling. The smallest group of about twenty, enclosed by fencing, was the closest to the house and barn. These were the cows Matt had decided to water at the stream. There was a pond to provide water closer than the stream, but Victoria didn't ask anything. She knew her father wanted to check the perimeter one more time.

They didn't talk on the way out. She knew what they were all thinking about. Her hand strayed to the rifle stock from time to time. All seemed normal until they drew closer to the stream. It hit her in an instant: there was more noise than usual. She could hear more cattle than the twenty head they were driving.

They exchanged glances and moved instantly. Victoria dug her heels into the mare's flank and shouted to urge her toward the rifle pit on the left. Alec came with her while Matt dashed toward the other rifle pit he'd constructed at the edge of the tree line. The war had started.

# Chapter 16
## *First Attack*

Victoria dove into the rifle pit just ahead of Alec, then rolled to get out of the way. The noise of the oncoming Erskine herd had alerted them just in time and kept them from riding into a tight spot. Cattle topped the rise in front of them in front of a wave of gunshots and loud yelling. Erskine's riders had stampeded the herd!

In the rifle pits and sheltered by oak trees, the Ridleys and Alec were protected from the stampede. Three riders appeared at the top of the rise behind the cattle, and Matt Ridley fired a quick shot—too quick. To her left, Alec muttered under his breath and held his fire. The riders ducked and scattered, offering little target to shoot at. All three were headed toward the position she now held with Alec in the rifle pit. Victoria knew her father's line of sight would be blocked by the cattle now.

Alec rose slightly and triggered a shot at the rider in front. His shot found its mark—the rider spun from his horse and narrowly avoided being trampled by the riders behind him. Too late, Alec saw a fourth man step from where he'd been behind a tree directly ahead. His answering shot knocked Alec backward, clutching at his shoulder.

Victoria fired at the shooter in the trees. A hat flew away, and she glimpsed a shock of red hair diving behind a tree. The two remaining riders on the slope ahead paused to fire at her as they retreated. Victoria dove back down into the cover of the rifle pit. When she risked a glance over the top, all the gunmen were gone, except for the one shot by Alec. He was crawling toward the edge of the pasture.

While she watched, the shooter with red hair galloped out from the trees, swung the man aboard behind him, spurred his horse through the cut wire at the top of the rise, and disappeared.

She turned to Alec, who was clutching his shoulder and struggling to rise. "They're gone," she said. "Stay down! We'll get you back to the house."

Alec slumped back to the ground, reaching with his good arm to pull his rifle in closer. Victoria dashed to her horse and came back with a small pack containing a knife, bandages, and tape. She used the knife to cut his shirt open, exposing the wound. She helped Alec come to a sitting position, and from there she could check the exit wound. The bullet appeared to have passed through.

Using the knife again, she cut a sleeve from Alec's shirt and another from her own shirt, using them to pack the wound and tie a bandage around his shoulder. A noise caused her to gasp, come to a half crouch, and reach for her rifle.

"Easy!" a voice commanded. "It's just me." Matt Ridley knelt beside them, covering the slope in front with his rifle. He glanced down at Alec. "Can you ride? We've got to get to the house before they come back."

Alec said nothing but struggled to his feet, still clutching his rifle with his left hand. Victoria reached out to take the rifle and guided him over to the horses. Her horse and Alec's had both stopped about thirty yards away, grazing. Matt followed them, still sweeping the slope and ridge above them, covering the retreat.

When they reached the horses, Matt gave Alec a leg up into the saddle. Alec moaned, leaned forward, and grabbed the saddle horn.

"You gonna make it?" Matt asked.

Alec nodded, answering through clenched teeth. "Ain't more'n half a mile. Jest get me back to the house, clean this out, and patch me up. I'll hold my own."

Matt ran to get his horse, then mounted up and trailed the other two back to the house. They found Margie Ridley in the corral, saddling up. She shaded her eyes, waved when she saw them, then left off saddling her horse and went to draw water from the well.

Victoria and Matt stood on either side of Alec, giving support as they walked him into the house. They peeled his shirt away and laid him on the table. When Margie bathed the wound, he moaned and passed out. Margie finished the job in silence.

Rusty, Victoria's brother, watched from the corner, resentment showing on his face. His father had refused to let him join them this morning on the ride to check the fence line. Victoria beckoned to her brother.

"We've got to get the horses closer to the house," she told him. "Come to the corral with me. We'll find a place where we can shelter them better. They're easy targets if these guys are low enough to shoot our horses."

Rusty brightened and led the way out the front door. "Behind the woodpile," he told her. "You'll see. Pa had me move some wood and drive some stakes into the ground. They'll have a hard time reaching them horses after we get 'em behind the woodpile."

They started by bringing over their own horses, with Rusty leading the way. When Victoria saw the preparations made by stacking the logs at the side of the house, she marveled again at how much her father had done to ready them for an attack.

The woodpile, which had run in a long, straight line parallel to the side of the house before, was in more of an L shape now. The pile turned inward at a sharp angle toward the house at one end, forming a shape like the bottom of an *L* and shielding the horses from fire. Any attackers would be exposed in an open pasture. Attacking from the rear would be slightly easier, but there would still be some treeless ground to cover before reaching the house.

Victoria shook her head in surprise. "When did you guys do this?" she asked.

Rusty shrugged. "Maybe two weeks ago. There's five stakes driven in back here. We can tether all our horses. All of 'em except the pack mule. He's on his own."

They made the return trip with Matt and Margie's horses, then Rusty ran back one more time for Alec's horse. He then helped unsaddle the three horses Victoria and the two men had ridden out to the stream this morning. Victoria saw Rusty notice the blood on Alec's saddle, but said nothing.

Victoria moved to join him, standing at the edge of the firewood pile and watching across the pasture. There was no movement.

"He won't let me help," Rusty blurted. "I'm as good a shot as he is. I been bringin' in game for the supper table for three years now. I can do something besides move logs and haul in water!"

Victoria reached to pat him on the shoulder. "He doesn't want you to get hurt, but you're growing up. I'll talk to him. I think our mom has something to do with it, too. You're the youngest, and she worries about you. I'll talk to her first, then I'll ask Dad to let you take a turn watching or something. I can't promise he'll listen to me, either, but I'll ask."

Rusty nodded gratefully and they linked arms as they walked back into the house.

"Remember this though," she told him on the way in, "the game wasn't shooting back. This might be different."

It was several hours later before she had the chance to talk to Matt about how they could proceed, taking shifts on watch. Alec had sipped some broth and fallen asleep in a chair, tossing and muttering now and then.

Margie served up a steaming bowl of stew for supper—there was no need to conserve food. They would run out of ammo before they would run out of food. The pump for water was close enough to the house to get water under cover of darkness, so they weren't worried about that.

Matt stood by the rifle slot cut into the door and peered out into the fading light. Victoria came to stand beside him. Margie was washing supper dishes in a large bowl nearby, with Rusty helping to dry and stack the dishes.

Victoria began the conversation in low tones. "We don't have enough people to get enough sleep and still keep watch during the night," she reminded him. Matt only shook his head and continued to stare through the slot in the door.

"You and me can take turns, then get a little extra shuteye when it gets light," he said. "Maybe Alec can help on another day."

Victoria stayed with it. "I had another thought, Dad," she said. "That pile of wood, the way you've got it stacked now, that's a good place to stand watch. Lots of cover. They won't be expecting anybody out there. I could go out there and watch, maybe in the middle of the night with the full moon coming over these next few days."

Matt turned to look at her, considering. "That's a good idea," he admitted grudgingly. "But you ain't goin' out there. I'll take that watch."

"Who's going to take turns with me in here?" she persisted. "We have to keep somebody at that door all night. Rusty can spell me. And who is going to watch your back and take turns with you out there? What if somebody slips past and gets in behind the woodpile?"

"I'll help watch outside." Both spun with surprise to see Margie walking over, drying her hands on a towel. "I'll help you, Matt. You let Rusty spell Victoria in here."

"I kin load," came a muffled voice from the chair. Alec had come awake and propped himself upright.

Matt shifted to stare at Alec, then his eyes moved from wife to son to daughter. He stared at the floor and sighed. "Wasn't supposed to be this way," he mumbled. He sighed again and looked at his family.

"It's a good plan," he said finally. "We'll try that for a night or two."

\* \* \*

Hawk raced his horse back toward the Erskine place, stopping only when his two unwounded men stopped to regroup. Hawk reined his horse to a stop, hearing moans from the wounded man riding double with him. He swung to face the others.

"Which one of you said you helped the doctors during the war? Carried sojers in to get patched up and stuff? One of you said you done that."

The one called Horne, a dark-haired man who said very little, edged his horse forward. "I done some of that," he admitted. It had kept him off the front lines for the last year of the war and maybe saved his life, but he didn't mention that.

Hawk motioned at him, and Horne moved his horse forward, then swung around to look at the injured man. He reached to pull the man's collar aside. Blood oozed from a place on the side of his neck. Horne leaned in for a closer look, then straightened up.

"He'll make it," he announced to Hawk. "Got hisself grazed pretty good on his neck, though. We need some bandages or clean rags or somethin' to stop the bleeding." He looked back at the wounded man.

"You okay, Collins?" he asked.

Collins grunted and concentrated on staying in the saddle.

"C'mon." Hawk led the way back to Erskine's ranch

house, leaving Collins to hang on as best he could. Five minutes later, they pulled up in front of the house. Erskine burst out the front door, glaring at nobody in particular. Hawk thought he smelled like whiskey. He glanced overhead. It was just about noon. Hawk like whiskey himself, but he had no use for a man that started drinking in the morning.

"I heard shootin'!" Erskine bawled at the top of his lungs. "Didja clear 'em out? They gone now?"

Hawk shook his head and stepped his horse forward, forcing Erskine to back up. "Nope," he said simply. "Not yet." He reached around and helped Collins swing down from his horse. "Got a wounded man here," he announced. "Gotta leave him here with you."

"You ain't leavin' him nowhere. Git back there and finish your job!" Erskine waved his arms in the air, belching when he backed up a step or two.

Hawk stared at him, considering. "Need some bandages, then, and some rags. Need some vittles, and we need to refill our canteens. We need another hoss for Collins here. We'll find his hoss later on."

"You'll git nuthin'! Git back there and finish the job. I don't wanna see you boys again until it's done. You can't git it done, I got somebody else that can!"

Hawk stared at him narrowly, then slowly dismounted. He stood facing Erskine and repeated his demands. His hand slid slowly down toward the pistol in his gun belt. The move wasn't lost on Erskine.

His face turning pale, Erskine backed away two more steps and held up a hand. "I'll getcha some beans from the kitchen and some rags. Go and get him a hoss from the corral. Not my bay gelding. Git another one."

He retreated toward his house. "Git your own water from the well," he yelled over his shoulder.

Ten minutes later, he came back out with a kettle of beans and some rags. While Hawk and his men ate, Erskine trotted out to the barn and came back with a box. He thumped it down on the ground. "Dynamite," he growled. "Do whatever you gotta do."

Hawk watched while Erskine retreated to the house. He walked over to inspect the dynamite while Horne wound a rag around Collins's neck. The other two men went to refill canteens.

In another ten minutes, they were all remounted. Collins swayed a little, but stayed in the saddle. Horne pointed at the box on the ground. "We gonna take that dynamite, boss?"

"Nope." Hawk glared toward the house. "I ain't usin' dynamite on 'em, women or no women. A man should have a fightin' chance." He stared at the ground and thought it over. "We'll go back and wait for dark," he decided. "We sneak up close to the house tonight and hit 'em first thing in the morning." He pointed at the box on the ground. "Take a couple sticks of dynamite. Maybe we can get 'em lookin' the wrong way when we come."

* * *

"Oh boy, here comes Doc Thomas and he's got a bead on you. You're in trouble now. Can't wait for this. You're his favorite, ya know."

Murph slurped out of his coffee mug and settled back to enjoy himself after telling me about the doc. I looked around and spotted him right away, set on a course for our table.

"You sure you didn't get hit on the head besides gettin' shot in the brisket?" Doc planted himself beside the table, hands on his hips while he glared at me. "I said you could go this morning, not yesterday. Where you been?"

"Mornin', Doc," I said. I pushed a cup at him. "Want some coffee? That's if Murph ain't drunk the whole pot yet."

I could have sworn there was a tiny little grin at the corner of Doc Thomas's mouth, but he just harrumphed a few times and settled himself in a chair. He fixed me with a glare while he poured some coffee. "You spring any more leaks while you was runnin' around and doing who knows what last night?"

"No, Doc." I was trying not to rile him up, on account of Murph telling me he wouldn't tell me where Victoria's ranch was unless the doc said I could go. "I been good. Just had me a glass of milk and went to bed early."

He glared at me again, and I decided some folks just can't see the humor in things. I looked over at Murph. He had his head down, grinning at his eggs. Doc Thomas clapped a paw on my forehead. "Got a fever?" He moved his paw around my forehead a few times and shook his head. "I guess not," he mumbled.

He shot another stare in my direction. "Headache? Stomach troubles? Not bleeding, you said?"

"No, Doc. No troubles at all. Not lately, I mean."

He snorted, which made him splutter into his coffee. He shook his head and glanced over at Murph.

"He can go. Just tell him to keep his fool head down next time they shoot at him."

"Right, I've been tryin' to tell him. He don't listen real good."

"You got that right," Doc mumbled under his breath and left. I think he maybe said something about getting paid in moonshine, but I can't be sure.

"What'd I tell you?" Murph snickered. "You're his favorite."

* * *

Our plan (before Doc Thomas interrupted us) was to get to the Ridley ranch by sundown. Not only did we not know what we might ride into, neither of us had ever been there, and all we had was the map Victoria had given to Murph. And what with the neighbors not gettin' along, we didn't think it was a good idea and stop and ask folks for directions along the way. We didn't want to do any of that after dark.

We moved along at a good pace, just stopping to water the horses when we came across a pond or stream. We ate in the saddle and kept going. Now and then, we checked the map Murph was carrying with him.

The shadows got a little longer the closer we got to that place on the map. We kept an eye out for the land-marks Victoria had drawn and kept pushing forward, but Murph finally pulled over and put the map away in his pocket.

"Gettin' too dark out here," he told me.

I guess he could see I wanted to keep going. He looked away, then pointed at a spot under some trees, maybe a hundred yards off the trail. "We could camp there."

I didn't answer, so he leaned in a little. "We don't know what we're riding into, you know. I don't care for ridin' up in the dark. They won't even know we're friends. They could have rustlers watching the place."

I knew he was right. "First light?" I asked. "If we're moving at first light, we could get there not much after dawn. That okay with you?"

Murph led the way off the trail to set up a small camp. "Okay with me," he called over his shoulder.

# Chapter 17
## *Raid at Dawn*

Hawk paced back and forth. His three men watched him, except for the wounded man, Collins. Collins had drifted off into a fitful sleep, lying in the shelter of a fallen log and surrounded by a stand of post oak trees. The bleeding from his wound had stopped, but Horne had warned him that a lot a movement would start things up again. Hawk figured Collins could come around enough to cover them from a sheltered position if they attacked the house. He wasn't counting on Collins for anything more than that.

The other two men besides Collins were wild cards. Erskine had hired them based on the small reputations they had as gunmen. Hawk had never seen them in action, and he really wasn't going to take Erskine's word on things. He didn't intend to risk his neck for any of them.

They had spent the afternoon and early evening watching the Ridley ranch house for any sign of activity. They'd seen nothing. The cattle had scattered. Clearly, nobody was herding the cows. He and his men were unlikely to run into anybody outside of that ranch house. The Ridleys were holed up in there. Hawk had used his binoculars to scan the layout of the place, and he had a vague plan that might work and still keep him out of danger.

Hawk had already ruled out approaching from the back or the west side of the house. There was too much open pasture out there on both sides. Cattle were grazing and would react to anybody approaching. There was no cover to be had—even the kid or either of the women could pick him off with ease if he came from either side.

That left the front of the house and the east side. There was enough cover from oak trees to get them close without being seen. A sudden rush might just get them close enough to take cover in the barn or corral and cut the Ridleys off from the well. Eventually, they would run out of water. A stick of dynamite set off near the house might scare them enough to get them to give it up and ride away. They had no way of knowing he wouldn't drop the dynamite down the chimney.

A dawn attack was always best, in Hawk's opinion. Just enough light to see where you're going without making too good a target of yourself. That just left the question of who would do what when they attacked the house at dawn.

Hawk liked the eastern side of the house for an attack, except for the stack of firewood. It was shaped suspiciously like a fort, from what he'd been able to see. It could make a great defensive position if they could get in there, or it could be a trap. He would let Horne and Collins come that side. Horne could attack, and Collins could give him cover.

That left a frontal attack for Hawk and the fourth man, a guy who almost never spoke. He carried a three-inch scar on his right cheek. Erskine had introduced him as Scar, and Scar had never bothered to give his real name. Hawk would let Scar lead the attack from the front. He could draw any unexpected fire, and Hawk would clean things up behind him.

Hawk left off his pacing and sat down to explain his plan to the group—it would be a dawn attack with Horne and Collins coming from the east side, and Hawk and Scar coming from the front. He left out the part about Scar going first to draw fire. He just said they would come from opposite ends of the house at the same time. Scar just shrugged and nodded.

Horne cocked his head and studied the plan Hawk had drawn out in the dirt with a stick. He glanced over at Collins, who was up and eating a little food now. Horne looked over at Hawk and made a request that surprised him.

"Dynamite," Horne said. "I want to have those sticks of dynamite we brought with us from Erskine's place. I can use 'em."

Hawk stalled by producing a cigar from his pocket and searching for a match while he thought that over. Eventually, he struck a match on his boot heel, lit the cigar, and took several puffs while staring at his drawing in the dirt.

He'd seen a lot of people blow themselves up in the war. Not everybody knew how to use that stuff. On the other hand, if he let Horne throw some dynamite around the time he attacked from the front, it would draw fire over to their side and away from him.

Hawk shrugged, went to his saddlebag, and pulled

out the sticks of dynamite. He handed them to Horne. "Best just to light it and throw," he advised. "Don't wait too long, but don't hold on so long they have a chance to throw it back at you."

Horne nodded and stuffed the dynamite in his saddlebag. Collins took a long drink of water from his canteen and said nothing. He had the simple job. He would just stay behind the trees and lay down a covering fire. Horne could blow himself up if he wanted to.

Hawk glanced overhead and pulled his Henry rifle from the scabbard. "We've got an hour to get into position. Just enough light to take cover before dark. Horne, you open the attack at dawn, whenever you've got enough light."

\* \* \*

Following Carl Erskine back to his ranch house had turned out to be a very easy job for Rex. Erskine hadn't turned to check his back trail even once. Rex grinned wryly at himself. It looked like this Erskine was a foolish man. Erskine should have realized Shade Taylor was a dangerous man to deal with.

Rex staked out a spot in the brush near the ranch house and watched for about two hours. Nobody came or went from the house. Erskine came out once to pump some water from the well. From the way he stumbled back and forth on the trip to the well, he needed the water to give him something to drink besides the whiskey he must be knocking down.

After two hours, Rex decided nothing important was going to happen at the Erskine house. He mounted and rode in the opposite direction from where he'd come, since he'd not seen signs of another ranch on the way over. The Ridley ranch must lie south of him.

He used trees and brush for cover until he was out of sight from the Erskine house, then moved out to follow a narrow trail through the pasture. He dismounted to look for recent travel, and it wasn't long before he spotted three sets of tracks.

Feeling a little wary now, Rex retreated to the trees and moved slowly, emerging once in a while to verify the tracks were still leading to the south. After moving from the trees back out to the trail and kneeling to check the tracks, he rose, shaded his eyes to look ahead, then froze where he stood.

There were three riders out there, dismounted and inspecting what appeared to be a wire fence. Rex quickly led his horse deep into the trees. When the riders stayed where they were, moving along the fence line on foot, he set up a small camp and unsaddled his horse. He might be here for a while.

* * *

Gunshots awakened Rex the next morning. He liked to brag that he was up at sunrise every day, but Rex hadn't seen a sunrise in quite a while. Not until this morning, that is. The gunshots brought him out of his blankets so suddenly that he banged his head on a tree limb above him.

Clapping a hand over his mouth to stop the volley of swearing that came to his lips, Rex staggered to the edge of the tree line and watched as the three Erskine riders fired their pistols and drove a herd of cattle through the place where a wire fence had been yesterday.

Staring, Rex could still see posts from the fence, but the wire was either gone entirely or hanging near the posts after the cattle had trampled it. While he watched, the cows disappeared over the ridge, followed by the riders.

He stood rooted where he was for just a minute, then ran back to camp to put on his pants and saddle his horse. Riding up near the fenceposts at the top of the ridge, he moved on foot to the edge of the ridge. Fresh gunshots greeted his ears. He saw an Erskine rider fall from his horse and start crawling toward the trees.

His decision made, Rex raced back to his horse and rode back to his campsite long enough to throw his bedroll over the saddle. He then put his heels to his horse and rode for the line cabin to tell Shade Taylor what had happened.

*  *  *

Victoria had taken the second watch inside the house at the slot in the front door. Her parents, Matt and Margie, had slipped outside to take posts in the firewood fort Matt had built with her brother Rusty. Victoria's eyebrows had risen when she saw her mother carrying a double-barreled shotgun out the door with her. She'd rarely seen her mother fire a weapon before, and certainly not at another person.

Before darkness had fallen, Matt had slipped outside and moved the horses to picket them behind the house. It was a risky move, but they couldn't afford to lose the horses, and none of them could stand the thought of a horse getting shot needlessly in a gunfire exchange. Matt had slipped back in without trouble.

At midnight, Rusty shook her shoulder to wake his sister, and they changed places. Rusty dozed off on a bedroll in the corner while Victoria watched through the gun slot at the front door. There was enough moonlight to see the outlines of the barn and corral, but nothing more. She placed a pot of coffee on the floor beside her and kept watch, wondering if there was really enough light to see anybody coming.

Inside the firewood fort, Matt placed himself at the corner facing the front pasture on one side and the woods to the east. He placed his wife at the opposite corner, on guard for an attack from the rear or the woods near the back side of the fort.

Margie placed the shotgun beside her and took up the watch. Matt watched her, saying nothing. He wondered if she would be able to pull the trigger if she needed to. It was a thought that stayed with him through the night. She knew what to do, he was sure of that. Pulling a trigger with a man in your sights is something else entirely.

* * *

It had taken them an hour to get into position near the firewood fort, but Horne was satisfied with where they'd settled in. He was a little worried about Collins. He'd started bleeding again on the way to get into place. Horne had stopped the bleeding with a little more bandaging and propped up Collins against a tree trunk, where he'd promptly dozed off. Horne would have to wake him up before they tried to get past that firewood and get next to the house.

The moonlight had been just enough to guide them in here—he'd been glad for it on the way in to this position. Now, though, he was worried they might be a little exposed. The trees gave some cover, but there were gaps in the brush. If there was anybody behind those logs, they could open fire without being seen.

As the night wore on, Horne started thinking there might really be somebody in position behind those logs. He had to admit it might be his brain playing tricks on him. The night was deathly quiet, though, aside from an occasional mockingbird making himself known. And Horne thought he might have heard people moving over there. Maybe even a whisper now and then. If somebody was whispering, how many people were in there?

They needed to wait until dawn before they could do anything, anyway. That was the plan they'd agreed on. At least, that was the plan Hawk had decided on and told them to follow. He might follow that plan, or he might not. If Horne saw a way to get in there before dawn, he would take it. But as the night crawled by, he decided it was best to wait for a little light.

Several times, he thought dawn was breaking, but he really had no way to tell the time out here. Finally, he felt certain he saw a little gray light filtering through the trees. Horne crawled over to make sure Collins was awake. He shook Collins gently, then clapped a hand over his mouth to keep him from calling out.

Collins's eyes flared open, then he relaxed and nodded when he recognized Horne, who crawled back over to take up his position. He'd made one decision during that long night. He was suspicious enough of somebody in position behind that firewood that he'd decided to use the dynamite. He would chuck a stick of it over the logs and duck. The wood would absorb most of the blast and then he would charge around what was left of the firewood.

He took his time, letting a little more light creep in before he reached into his saddlebag and pulled out a match. Horne pulled the dynamite to him and turned to shield the wick from the slight breeze blowing in from the south.

He held the match to the wick and saw it spark and catch on. Horne waited just a moment, then rose to a crouching position, lifted the dynamite, and prepared to throw it over the woodpile. He felt the crash in his chest before he heard the boom of the shotgun.

\* \* \*

Margie Ridley eased her position and stretched to relieve the stiffness in her back. She had cleared a little spot at the top of the firewood stack to rest the barrel of the shotgun. She could shift the butt of the gun back and forth to get a good view of the trees in front of her. Several hours had gone by, and she'd seen nothing out there, but she didn't really expect to see much before morning.

Margie had used the shotgun a few times to shoot turkeys for food, or maybe wild hogs that were digging up her garden. She'd never thought she could fire it at another person, but she knew this last year had changed her.

Everything they had was tied up in this ranch. It was for Margie and Matt to have in their old age, and it was the inheritance to pass on to their children. Land had been hard to come by back east, and she didn't take this for granted. She would fight for it. She sighted down the barrel for about the fiftieth time that night and shifted the butt back and forth, watching the woods.

When she saw a brief flicker of light, she couldn't believe her eyes at first. She started to call out to Matt, then clamped her mouth shut. If there was somebody right out there in front of her, it was up to her to deal with it.

At first, there was just that flicker of light, then nothing. Then she saw sparks and a bigger flame. She saw shadows moving, then a low, thin object seemed to be rising in the air, sparking from one end. She saw the dark outline of a man just before she squeezed off both triggers.

The blast of the shotgun was deafening. She was driven back and landed on the ground. The shotgun fell at her feet. Just as the roar of the shotgun died away, there was another huge explosion.

* * *

Collins watched as Horne lit the dynamite. He pushed himself to a crouching position, still leaning back against a post oak tree. He felt confident he could lay down a good fire to cover Horne.

He saw the flicker of flame, then he saw Horne raising the dynamite. Collins shifted his gaze to the woodpile, alert for any movement. Then he heard the unmistakable crash of a shotgun. He looked back at Horne, who was stumbling backward before he collapsed on the ground. The dynamite landed near him, still sparking and burning.

Collins gasped and launched himself toward the dynamite. He tripped and landed face-down, then pushed himself back up and lunged to get the explosive before it was too late. If only he could throw it...he didn't make it.

\* \* \*

Matt Ridley was watching the open field in front of him in the early light, using the corners of his eyes to help him catch movement, like they'd taught him in the Army. He was aware of nothing happening behind him until the roar of the shotgun tore open the morning quiet.

Matt wheeled to see Margie staggering backward and landing on the ground. There was an enormous explosion, and then the entire side wall of the firewood fort collapsed inward. Matt rushed to pull Margie away from the falling logs. He kneeled beside her.

"I'm okay," she murmured. "Get the shotgun out from under those logs."

Stunned by the explosion, Matt reached to get the shotgun. He handed it to Margie. She knew how to reload it and was already doing that. His gut told him there was no threat left out there on the east side. If the attackers hadn't been killed, they were in no shape to attack.

Matt rushed back to his position at the front of the firewood pile. Gunfire broke out ahead of him. They were coming through the pasture, rushing the house. He steadied his rifle on top of the logs and waited to get a clear shot. Margie moved up to stand beside him, shotgun ready.

Matt didn't have to wonder if Victoria was alert and on duty at the front door. There was no chance she hadn't heard the explosion. If they charged the front door, they would get a hot reception.

# Chapter 18
## *Just in Time*

We split up when Victoria's map told us we'd reached the edge of the Ridley's property. Things were way too tense around there right now to ride up to the house with dawn just breaking. Victoria and her family would have to figure that anybody riding up to the house without announcing himself as a friend might just be an enemy.

Dismounted, Murph went toward the east, and I worked my way west, cat-footing it through the trees and brush until I could make out the outline of the ranch house, sitting across a broad pasture and behind what looked like a corral and barn.

I broke out my binoculars and scanned the buildings. There was no sign of activity, and I figured that was bad. A ranch family was likely to be up and out by daybreak, looking after the animals and doing chores. I was sure they'd be up, but they didn't feel safe coming outside.

I had agreed with Murph to meet up after about an

hour at the place where we parted ways this morning. By then, we expected to have a better feel for what was happening down there, and we would make one last sweep of these woods before crossing that pasture and approaching the house.

It's hard to say what alerted me to the guy sitting on his horse just about thirty or forty yards to my left. He was sitting perfectly still at the corner of my vision when I realized somebody was over there. I eased my gaze to the left for a better look. Maybe he had shifted just a little, and I'd picked up the motion. He would have a good shot at me with that Henry he had cradled in his arms if he looked this way and took a notion to fire.

He also had some kind of old spyglass in one hand, and he was staring across the pasture at the ranch house. When he lifted the spyglass for a closer look, I eased back to get a little cover from a tree just behind me.

I wondered if he had any buddies out here in these woods, and if he did, was Murph about to run across one of 'em? There were about a hundred thoughts going through my head when an explosion erupted near the house. I swung to look and saw dust and flames coming from the trees next to the house. A woodpile was standing between the house and the trees, and some of it started to crumble.

The guy I'd been watching over to my left moved, and I turned in time to see him lift the rifle and urge his horse forward. He was intent on the house and the explosion.

"Hold it!" I stepped out from behind the tree, lifting

my brand-new Winchester and laying the sights on his chest.

He froze for just a second, then wheeled around, trying to bring the Henry to bear on me. All I had to do was pull the trigger. I didn't even have to think about it. He slumped back in the saddle, laying across the horse's shoulders, then his horse bolted across the pasture. He fell from the saddle, bounced a time or two, then came to a rest.

I raced back to get my horse before I heard one shot, then a second, coming from somewhere over in the area Murph had gone to scout. I jump aboard Cisco and knew I had to decide right now. Should I ride to the house to check on the Ridleys, or go to help Murph? I chose the Ridleys. Murph knew what to do in a fight. I had to hope he wasn't outnumbered.

I rode Cisco to the edge of the tree line, then moved him out a few steps into the pasture. I took off my hat and waved it in the air, but stayed low in the saddle and away from the gunshots I'd heard on my left. I needed Victoria to see me in the house without presenting myself as a target. It was a bad moment.

Somebody opened the front door of the house, waved, then stepped back inside. It was Victoria! There was more movement by that woodpile on the left side of the house. A man and woman stepped from behind the logs, rifle and shotgun pointed up in the air. They waved as well.

I put my heels to Cisco and took him across the pasture at a gallop, swinging down just a few yards short of the house.

* * *

Rex hadn't exactly been invited to stick around at the line cabin after he reported the fence cutting and stampede yesterday afternoon. Shade Taylor had stared at him, talked back and forth with his buddy Eli for a minute, then told Rex to get back over there and keep an eye on things. Rex had done that, but only after getting himself something to eat and packing a little food in his saddlebag. Shade Taylor had glared at him until he got out of the cabin and back on his horse.

Now, nestled into his blankets, he had a feeling there was going to be some shooting in the morning. He'd not been able to pick up a recent trail for the four Erskine riders, but he had a feeling that was because they were all tucked away, hidden out in positions they could use for an attack on the Ridley ranch in the morning. They weren't likely to move until then.

Rex's own spot was comfortably away from the Ridley ranch house. In fact, he was about halfway between the stream where the Ridleys watered their cattle and their house. He was a little closer to the trail than he would have liked, but he was still back in the trees. From here, he could be on the trail and gone in a hurry if he needed to. He had no intention of getting into the middle of this fight.

His bad habit of sleeping until the sun was high above caused a problem the next morning. He was still snoring loudly when the first shots rang out. He rolled over and mumbled in his sleep, then started to drift off again. When the dynamite blew up, he cursed, leaped from his blankets, and searched wildly for his pants.

He found the pants and was reaching for his boots when a shot rang out. It sounded uncomfortably close.

A second shot rang out as he was pulling on his boots. He left his blankets on the ground and was running for his horse when he heard hoofbeats coming up behind him. He whirled to see a man he didn't recognize bearing down on him. He threw his hands in the air as the man drew his pistol.

The first shot caught him in the middle of his forehead. He never felt the second shot as he slumped to the ground. He was only aware of the sunlight overhead fading away.

Hawk didn't know the guy he'd just shot, and he didn't care about that. He knew there was somebody with a badge on his tail. He'd stopped long enough to see the man following his tracks. He just knew he needed to clear out. His odds had dropped way below where he liked them when two of his men had blown up in the woods and another got gunned down in front of him.

Hawk rode past the dead man without looking down. He wouldn't bother stopping at the Erskine ranch on his way out. He needed to catch a train. It didn't really matter which way the train was headed. The farther away, the better.

* * *

I swung down from Cisco, and Victoria came running at me, then jumped to wrap her arms around me in a hug. I staggered back against Cisco, but managed to stay on my feet. My brain was trying to deal with too many things at once. The main thought, though, was that if I'd known I would get this kind of welcome, I would have found a way to come sooner.

A man and woman came around from behind a woodpile at the side of the house. Then a younger guy came out of the house. I knew I must be seeing the rest of the family—Matt and Margie and younger brother Rusty. The red hair gave him away.

I was mighty happy to see that Matt still had his rifle at the ready, scanning the far edges of the pasture and the tree line. Murph was still out there somewhere, and I had heard shots coming from that way a little while ago.

Alec came out of the house, endured the fussing Margie made over him, and took a seat on the bench outside. He nodded at me and cradled a rifle across his lap. I could see he'd been bandaged up.

Margie came over and gave me a brief hug. Matt offered me a handshake, then Rusty clapped me on the shoulder and gave me a handshake as well. "Well," I mumbled, not used to anything like this, "I feel like some kind of hee-ro."

Victoria pulled my head down and kissed my cheek. "You are a hero," she said. "I don't know what we would have done if you hadn't showed up."

I looked over past the woodpile, where at least one tree had been knocked down, and there was another leaning way over, and smoke was still rising. "Looks like you've been doing a pretty fair amount of shooting on your own," I observed. "What happened over there?"

Matt shook his head. "They were gonna throw a stick of dynamite, I guess. We, uh..." he looked over at Margie, who was staring at the ground. She was holding a shotgun, and I could guess the rest. Matt didn't finish his thought.

I could see that nobody here had the stomach to go

over and see what had happened in those trees. "You keep watch on the tree line and pasture," I told Matt. "My friend Murph, who is a Ranger, is out there somewhere. I'll look for him in a bit."

"What do I need to do?" Victoria had reached out to grab my arm.

I nodded at Margie, who was still staring at the ground. "I think your ma could use some help," I told her.

When I moved over to the spot where the dynamite had gone off, I could barely hold down my breakfast. Two men had been blown up over here, and there wasn't a lot left of them. I could only guess they were two of Erskine's gun hands. I scouted around for a bit, then returned to the Ridleys.

Victoria had gone inside with her mother. Matt and Rusty were keeping watch outside, along with Alec, who was still sitting on the bench.

"I'll be back in a bit," I told them. "Two men died over there. There's no sign of anybody else. I'll bury them as best I can when I get back. Right now, I need to ride out there and see what's become of Murph."

* * *

The chase through the woods had been a short one for Murph. When all the excitement had erupted a little earlier, he had been working his way toward the pasture. He'd reined in after a dynamite explosion, then somebody had been gunned down off to his right. He'd gotten a good enough look to know Walker hadn't gone down from that shot. That meant Walker had shot one of Erskine's riders.

Right after that, somebody on horseback had burst past him, surprisingly close. The man hadn't been looking left or right—he was just moving in a hurry. About a minute later, Murph heard a couple more gunshots.

Murph moved in behind the gunman, pushing his horse to catch up. After a while, he changed his mind and slowed down. This was a prime place to ride into an ambush, and Murph didn't fancy that. He still followed the tracks, but now he paused often to look and listen.

When he came across a dead man in the woods, he knew he'd found out what the gunshots in front of him had been all about. Murph dismounted warily and waited. Satisfied after a couple minutes that the shooter had moved on, Murph went to check on the body lying at the base of the tree.

After checking for a heartbeat and finding none, Murph stood and absently slapped his hat against his thigh. A breeze through the trees and the branches moving above left a strange pattern of sunlight moving over the dead body. He remounted and followed the tracks for another ten minutes, but he knew his quarry had put a lot of distance between them by now.

Returning to the dead man, Murph checked around and found the man's horse tied to a tree limb nearby. Murph led the horse over and loaded the dead man over the horse, tying the man's hand underneath the horse's belly.

From there, he struck a path toward the pasture and the ranch house. Pausing at the edge of the pasture, he could see Nash Walker and the girl, along with a few other folks, standing in front of the house. Murph stopped and waved his hat over his head, then proceeded in.

* * *

I didn't have much stomach for dealing with those blown-up bodies over there in the trees, but the Ridleys had less of a stomach for it than I did. Victoria offered to help, but I couldn't ask her to do that. I just shook my head.

"I guess I'll find a shovel in the barn?" I asked Matt. He looked at Rusty. "Go out there and find him a shovel," he said.

Rusty trotted off. Matt shielded his eyes and looked out at the pasture. "I guess there's another grave to dig," he said, pointing at the body off to my left and out in the pasture. I had forgotten about shooting the guy out there near the trees.

"Right," I said. "Two graves." Just then, I saw somebody waving a hat and riding out of the woods. It was Murph, leading a horse with another body strapped over the top of it. "Three graves," I corrected myself.

Murph rode up, and Victoria made introductions all the way around. "Thank you for coming," she said to Murph, giving him a hug. He shook his head.

"I barely kept him from gettin' off his deathbed to git here," he said, pointing at me. "I had to ride along just to save his hide. There's a doc back in Austin that don't want him for a patient no more."

Victoria stared at me. "You got hurt? At that Taylor place?"

Well, sir, after that, I had to tell the story about

Shade Taylor and JW Hardin. None of the Ridleys had heard of those two, but they'd all heard tell about the Taylor-Sutton feud. Victoria took the shovel away from me and said I wouldn't be doing any digging today.

After that, Murph and I went to the woods where the dynamite had gone off and did what we could to clean things up. I dug a time or two when Victoria wasn't looking, and we got it fixed up to where the first good rain would wash away what was left of the mess.

Victoria came and stood guard with the shotgun while Murph, Matt, Rusty, and I took Murph's dead guy out to bury him along with the man I had shot when all this got started early this morning. It seemed like a very long time ago.

We led the dead man's horse with Murph's guy still draped over it to the edge of the woods and dropped him off there. Murph asked if anybody had seen this guy, and everybody shook their heads.

Matt dragged the man I'd shot over, and Murph asked the same question. Everybody said no except for Rusty, who stood and looked for a while. "I've seen that scar," he said. "Hard to forget that. I've seen this guy up near the fence line. He's one of Erskine's hands."

Murph pushed his hat back on his head and sighed. "Okay," he announced. "Let's get these boys buried. Nash, you can't dig 'cause your sweetheart over there says so. You can just watch and act like you're important around here."

Victoria blushed a deep red, and I glared at Murph, who paid no attention. I noticed that Matt and Rusty went on grinning for quite a while.

The ground was wet from recent rains, so the

digging went pretty fast. Nobody seemed to have any good words to say over them, so we just finished it up and went back to the house, where everybody gathered in the front room.

I looked at Matt. "I'll be here for as long as you folks need me," I told him. "I can't speak for Murph, but what do you need me to do now?"

Matt cleared his throat and pulled at his chin for a moment. "Well," he drawled, "them cows is scattered from here to breakfast, what with that stampede and all. We could sure use some help rounding them up and returning Erskine's cows." He paused and thought about that. "I ain't exactly sure if he'll be neighborly if I try to return 'em."

Murph took over. "I'll stay and help round 'em up. Let me and Nash drive 'em up to the Erskine ranch. He won't shoot at a badge if he's got a right mind on his shoulders. I need to have a talk with him, anyway."

"What about keeping watch here?" I asked.

Alec rose from the corner, walked over, and took a seat at the table. "I can still shoot," he said.

Margie insisted on feeding everybody before we went out to start rounding up cows. I was surprised to find out it wasn't even noon yet. I tried to remember some table manners when the food came. I didn't have too many of those, but I ate with my fork and kept both feet on the floor. I don't guess I embarrassed myself too much. Margie looked pleased when I agreed to seconds on everything.

It took the rest of the day to round up cattle and get 'em to the pastures where Matt wanted them. The Ridleys insisted that Murph and I should stay for dinner, then Murph and I went out to bunk in at the barn.

"Come mornin'," Murph told me. "We take them Erskine cows up to his place. Look sharp and keep that new Colt of yours handy."

# Chapter 19
## *Levi's Return*

Carl Erskine was sitting on his front porch when we drove about forty head of cattle into his front pasture. He stayed where he was while we closed a gate on the pasture fence and rode toward the porch. Erskine didn't move except to take a swig from a flask. He watched with bleary eyes while we took seats.

There was a long silence. Erskine finally put his flask away and scratched his belly. "You brung me some cows," he mumbled softly. "Thanksh. They strayed this mornin', I guess. Had some hands leave me an' I couldn't bring 'em back."

A short, wiry man stepped around the corner and moved behind Erskine. "This here's Duffy," he said. "He's my foreman." Erskine swayed a little and thought it over. "He's my only hand now, I guess." He pointed at the cattle we had just put in the front pasture. "Take a look at them cows, Duffy. Move 'em to where they can get some water."

Duffy nodded, mounted his horse, and moved out to the corral.

"Where's your other hands?" Murph asked. "You don't have enough to run this place unless you've got more than one cowboy."

Erskine broke out the flask again and took a long swallow. "There was some others. They all quit on me. Day before yesterday." He stared bleakly while Duffy drove the cows away from the house. "Up and quit, all of 'em," he mumbled.

"Where have you been this morning?" Murph asked, changing the subject suddenly.

Erskine shrugged. "Been right here. Just waitin' for Duffy to come out so we can tend to the cows."

Murph exchanged glances with me and shrugged in frustration. "You ever have a cowboy with a big ugly scar on his right cheek?" he asked suddenly. "A cowboy or a gunhand, whichever it was."

Erskine's eyes seemed to flicker for a moment, then he slumped down in his chair and shook his head. "Nope," he growled. "Never had nobody workin' like that around here."

"How many hands quit?" Murph said, leaning forward to stare at him.

Erskine thought that one over before answering, "Four quit. Only Duffy ain't quit on me," he said after a pause.

"Now ain't that interestin'," Murph said sharply. "We've got four dead men over at your neighbor's place this morning. You know, the Ridley place? Two of 'em got themselves shot, and the other two blew themselves up with dynamite. It was a mess."

Erskine reached for the flask one more time. "Don't know nuthin' about that," he insisted. "Them boys that worked for me rode away the day before yesterday. They wasn't worth much, anyway."

Murph stood suddenly, jammed his hat on his head, and motioned at me. "I'll likely be back," he told Erskine. "I'll make sure I have somebody checkin' on you from time to time. We better not see any brands that don't belong to you."

Erskine said nothing. He stayed slumped in his chair while we rode out.

"He's behind this," Murph growled. "I can't prove anything. Ridley was talking this morning, though, about taking some cows to Austin for sale. You and me need to be on that drive, and I'll get somebody else out here to watch the Ridley place for a while. Carl Erskine might just have somethin' else up his sleeve."

\* \* \*

Shade Taylor heard the cattle before he and Eli saw the riders coming. They pulled off the trail between the Erskine and Ridley ranches and watched from cover while a Texas Ranger and the guy Shade recognized as Nash Walker drove several dozen head past. The Erskine brand was clear on the cows as they passed. Shade guessed the riders were returning the cows that had been stampede onto Ridley land.

They had heard the explosion clear down at the line cabin this morning. Shade and Eli had mounted up right away and ridden toward the Ridley place. Shade had expected to see Rex galloping back to report what had happened. Shade suspected the worst when Rex never showed.

The remains of a barbed wire fence were hanging

from some fenceposts at the top of a rise on the trail. Shade's instinct had told him not to ride past the fenceposts. It was clear that Erskine's hands had cut that wire and they hadn't come back. When the Texas Ranger and Nash Walker came by a while later, driving Erskine cattle, it hadn't been that hard to figure some things out.

There had been a fight here this morning between Erskine's gunhands, the Ranger, and Nash Walker. Maybe Ridley had somebody else helping him as well. Erskine's hands were nowhere to be seen and Walker and his pal were openly driving the cattle home. That meant that Erskine's hand had been killed or scattered.

"Whaddya think?"

Eli had held his silence for several minutes after the cattle passed. Shade Taylor leaned over to spit.

"Well, I don't think Erskine's got any hands left. Somebody got blowed up along with some dynamite, I'm guessin'." He sat a moment longer, then moved out through the woods toward the Ridley ranch.

"Let's just take a look and see where that explosion went off. Then, I think we can go see Erskine. He might just be in a mood to give us everything we want if we can do what his boys didn't get done. It don't really matter, though. We can just take what we want now. He's got nobody left."

Eli could do the numbers in his head. They had only two guns to at least three or four for Ridley. He knew the answer to that one, though. Shade had no intention of fighting fair. That was okay with Eli. When you dry-gulched somebody from a hideout, nobody was shooting back.

Twenty minutes later, they were riding back to see

Erskine. They had seen everything they needed to see down there. The explosion had obviously gone off in the woods next to the house. There were a couple of fresh graves here and there, and Ridley and his daughter were moving around in the corral. An old guy with a rifle across his lap was guarding the house.

"Doesn't look like they lost nobody," Eli observed.

Shade only grunted and kept riding. They stayed in the woods and moved slowly, so as not to run into the Ranger and Walker on their way back.

\* \* \*

Their next stop was obvious. Shade and Eli rode up to the Erskine ranch house, dismounted, and took seats on the front patio without an invitation from Erskine.

"You guys, too," Erskine mumbled. "I got all kinds of company this mornin' and I didn't want none of it." Shade and Eli waited for something else, but Erskine was done talking. Shade leaned forward.

"Your boys are done," Shade growled. "Either kilt or skedaddled. I guess maybe you know about that." He paused. Erskine still had nothing to say. Shade Taylor pressed him. "You done lost that range war in one day. Unless Eli and me straighten things out for you."

Finally, there was a flicker of interest from Erskine. He stared at them, then picked up a jug and passed it over. "I'm listenin'." He leaned back and looked at them for the first time.

"We go down to that ranch over there and take over. Me and Eli. We move 'em out and take the place. You get to use that stream to water your cows as much as you need if you keep your mouth shut. That's it. We take the land, the house, the cattle, everything."

Erskine paused with a flash halfway to his mouth and spluttered. "You take everything?" His voice rose, and the flask fell into his lap. "That ain't a deal. That's just robbing me!"

"What else kin you do?" Shade leaned back and put his hands behind his head, his lips set into a sneer. "You got nobody left except that old man that herds cows for you. You gonna do the fighting yourself?"

Erskine wiped his mouth with the back of his sleeve. "I can hire more guns," he protested. "That's what I can do."

"They gonna do any better than this lot?" Shade pointed toward the Ridley place. "Looks like they blew themselves up with their own dynamite. Four of 'em got beat by two men and an old stove-up ranch hand."

Shade leaned in again. "Plus, you'd have to pay new hands. We won't charge you nuthin'. You get the water you need to run your cows. It'll save your ranch. That place ain't yours to give. You just keep your mouth shut about what happens to them folks. Think about it."

Shade rose, and Eli stood with him. They moved toward their horses.

"Okay, deal." Erskine stood, shoulders slumped, with defeat in the lines of his face. "I don't wanna hear nothing about what you do down there. I got nuthin' to do with that. You get the ranch and cows. I don't tell nobody." He extended a shaking hand.

"Deal." Shade Taylor nodded. He ignored Erskine's hand.

* * *

After another great dinner from Margie and Victoria, Matt Ridley told us more about what he had on his mind. He'd been wanting to sell off some of his stock to raise a little money, but he'd been afraid of leaving the ranch long enough to do it.

Now, he leaned his elbows on the table and looked across the table at Murph and me. "You boys are goin' back to Austin anyway, right?" he asked. I could see where this was going. I didn't mind driving his cows, and I knew Murph had already decided to go. He had a job that didn't include herding cows, but this was about ending a range war.

We were all watching Murph. He reached for another piece of apple pie. "I've got a man comin' out here in a day or two," he said. That surprised me.

"I told one of my men to come out here if I wasn't back in a couple days," he explained. "I had a bad feeling about things out here." He stopped to shovel down a few mouthfuls of pie. "So," he went on, "when my man Hoskins gets here to help look after this place for a couple days, I'll be headed home. I don't mind driving a few cows back to Austin with me."

"We don't need anybody to watch this place," Matt Ridley objected, but Margie reached out to put a hand over his.

"We can use the help for a few days," she said. "Besides, I have a feeling one of us might want to go back to Austin with you. That would leave us a hand short around here." She glanced across the table at Victoria. "Alec's doing better, but he's not all the way on his feet yet."

Victoria looked across the table and smiled at me. I

was liking the idea of this cattle drive to Austin better all the time. All eyes turned to Matt.

Matt looked around the table and threw his hands in the air. "I done been outvoted again," he decided. "We can pick out the cows we wanna sell in the morning. I can have 'em ready to go as soon as your man arrives."

\* \* \*

Matt and Rusty made short work of rounding up the cattle he wanted to sell in Austin. Murph mostly watched the woods and trail while Victoria and I lent a hand and a lasso now and then.

By noon, we had assembled a herd of fifty head, mostly mixed breed. More than half were steers, and the rest were cows. There was a mixed-breed longhorn that Matt thought might serve as a bell cow for us.

Murph, watching the tree line, sat up in his saddle and reached toward his rifle. "Riders coming in!" he announced. I drifted over to my Winchester, leaning against the rails in the corner of the corral.

"It's Hoskins!" Murph called. He stared out across the pasture. "It's Hoskins, and he's got a friend with him." Moments later, he leaned forward in his saddle. "Well, I'll be...he's got an old buddy of yours with him, Walker."

Within a few seconds, I recognized the second rider. I don't know why I hadn't figured it out sooner. After all, I'd ridden all the way from Tennessee to Texas with him. It was Levi Noone. No telling where that guy was likely to show up.

\* \* \*

Covered by thick oak trees and underbrush, well back into the trees, Shade Taylor studied the corral of the Ridley ranch. Eli was waiting silently, swaying a little as the horse stamped his feet. After several minutes, Shade lowered his binoculars and cursed softly.

"One of them that just come in is another lawman, just like we thought when he rode past here. That glint off his chest is a badge, for sure. Either another Ranger or a sheriff from somewhere, I expect. Dunno who the other one is that rode in with him." He leaned over to spit.

"Can't figure out why Walker is in the corral. I know him...just didn't expect to see him here. Don't know what he's doin' out here. Maybe he's sweet on that girl."

"Who is he?" Eli didn't want to set off Shade Taylor's famous temper, but he'd had enough of waiting for Taylor to explain things.

Shade shook his head. "Name's Nash Walker. I rode with him some out at the Creed Taylor ranch. Left him in some brush a while back, thought he might be dead. He'd taken at least one bullet...guess he got himself out of that mess."

He pushed his hat back and scratched his chin thoughtfully. "We can't do anything here right now. There's two badges down there, and that Nash Walker is pretty handy with either rifle or pistol. I taught him some myself. He took down one of my boys, and it was some pretty good shootin'."

Shade reined his horse around, and they started back for the line cabin on Erskine's property. "They're gathering up cows like they're gonna drive 'em some-where and sell 'em. We can tag along and maybe take out Walker and the other guy that ain't a Ranger. That would make for a nice start on things."

\* \* \*

We were well down the trail to Austin before the sun was up very far in the sky the next morning. Murph rode out front, rifle at the ready. He said he still had a bad feeling about this range war we had just left behind. Levi rode on one flank and Victoria on the other. That left me riding drag at the rear. I knew that was the worst job on a drive, but we didn't have enough cows to kick up too much dust.

Levi Noone had said something this morning before we left to explain why he'd come out here with Hoskins. He was working, still making money doing bounty hunting. He'd had a tip that his latest quarry had come out this way. Somebody named Eli Perkins. He asked if I'd heard of him. I just shook my head. It didn't ring any bells.

Nobody else had heard of him either, so when Levi learned about the four dead guys we'd just buried at the Ridley place, he decided Eli Perkins was likely to be one of them. He was going back to Austin to get the name of another guy to bring in.

We moved along without any big problems, which was a relief for all of us. Matt had provided an old wagon that passed for a chuck wagon, along with a couple of extra horses. We were in the saddle early and broke for camp in the early evening. We had figured it would take us four days, and we looked to be right on track after two.

We made camp a little early that second night after we came to a good stream for watering the cattle and horses. Levi shot a deer, and he and Murph were dressing the doe while I tended to the horses and Victoria got a fire going to cook the venison.

After dinner, Levi and Murph turned in early while I helped Victoria clean up after the meal. Then we went over to lean back against a fallen log while the campfire burned down. With the Texas sky full of stars and the flickering light from the fire, things were getting pretty cozy. Then Victoria snuggled up close to me. I didn't know where this was going, but I liked it so far.

"What's next for you after we get to Austin?" she asked.

That surprised me a little. I thought the both of us would go back to the ranch to make sure things were okay, but Victoria shrugged when I mentioned it. "I might not be going back," she told me. "Hoskins will keep an eye on things for a while, and Alec will be back on his feet soon. My folks know I might just catch the train to Dallas and then a stagecoach with the other people in the show. They're going out to Denver soon."

I had to think about that for a while. I'd had it in my mind to buy a few cows and pitch in with Goodnight for a drive to Colorado, but was this the time? I hadn't thought I would be ready this soon.

She was reading my mind. "What about going with Charles Goodnight and driving some cows up the Goodnight-Loving Trail?" she asked. "You've talked about that before. If you went now, how many cows could you buy for the drive?"

That made me do some ciphering in my head, which took a while. Besides that, I was kinda distracted by the two of us being all snuggled up behind that log. Finally, I came up with a number.

"About twenty, I think. I guess that would be worth my while."

Victoria thought that one over. "How about if I lend you some money and you can buy another twenty cows? You could drive them to Denver, sell them, and then meet me up there."

A smile spread across my face. "I like that plan. A lot." That grin wouldn't stop. I think it reached my ears.

"Good." Victoria got up on her knees, took my face in both her hands, and planted a kiss on my lips. "Good night," she whispered. "We can talk more about Denver." With that, she went and rolled up in her blankets.

I stayed for a while, leaned up against that log with my hands behind my head, staring up at the stars. I couldn't wait to go up to Ft. Worth and look for Charles Goodnight.

# Chapter 20
## *Austin Streets*

Eli Perkins had been a saddle partner with Shade Taylor on an off-and-on basis for almost five years. When Shade had signed on with the Creed Taylor ranch, Eli had decided to rustle cattle in Mexico for a while. He'd heard some bad things about that Taylor-Sutton feud. He didn't mind the rustling, he just wasn't quite as greedy as Shade. When Shade left the Taylor ranch, Eli had run across him in an Austin saloon a few weeks ago and joined forces with him again.

They were in that same Austin saloon now, fresh off the trail from the Erskine ranch, after shadowing the cattle drive made by Nash Walker, a Texas Ranger and two others. Eli had seen Shade in a bad mood a lot. Maybe most of the time he'd seen Shade in a bad mood. Right now, though, Shade Taylor was like a grizzly bear with a sore tooth.

When they had started the trip, they had agreed they wouldn't try to dry-gulch a group with both a Texas Ranger and a girl in it. If anybody survived to tell that story, they wouldn't be safe anywhere in the West.

Even so, Eli had talked Shade out of dry gulching Nash Walker several times on the trip.

Now, sitting in the saloon, Shade was talking more craziness. Still, it didn't sound as dangerous to Eli as the nonsense Shade had been talking on the trip into Austin. Shade was talking about facing down Nash Walker here in Austin, only he wasn't talking about a fair fight. He just needed it to look like a fair fight. A shootout in the street, where everybody could see it.

Eli looked at Shade, trying to make sure he'd heard things right. "You want me to be in a loft in the livery barn?" Eli asked. He shaded his eyes to look at the barn Shade was pointing at, just down the street.

"Right." Shade drained his third glass of whiskey and waved for another. "I'll call out Walker in the street out there." He pointed again. "He and that girl went to that café over there right after they sold their cows, so sooner or later he'll come out on the street with the girl."

Shade stopped while the waiter brought a fresh glass of whiskey for him and a beer for Eli. "You'll be up in that barn. I'll prob'ly beat him anyway, but I just want you to make sure. You fire just as soon as we draw. It'll be my shot that kills him, but you just make sure." He drained another glass.

Eli sipped his beer. He needed a cool head now. He stared out at the street, then up at the loft in the livery stable. "How much?" he asked. "How much to be up there and cover your back? And what about the girl?"

Shade stopped in mid-slurp. A shocked expression crossed his face. "You'd make me pay you for that? I'm your saddle partner!"

Eli shrugged. "If anybody figgers out what I did, I'll get my neck stretched for it. So yeah, you'd have to pay me." He paused. "Five hunnerd dollars. And what about the girl?"

Shade Taylor's jaw dropped open for the second time in the last minute. "Five hunnerd?? Dollars?? He scowled and made a sweeping motion with his hand. We won't hit the girl. She'll git outta the way."

Eli shrugged, then nodded grimly. It'll be my neck in the noose and not yours if anybody finds out it wasn't fair. What you're doin' won't get nobody riled up like a dry gulchin'."

Ten minutes, two beers, and three whiskeys later, they agreed on three hundred dollars. They would make sure they didn't shoot the girl. Shade Taylor threw some money on the table and stormed out of the saloon. Eli finished his beer slowly, stepped out of the saloon, and strolled past the sheriff's office. If he had looked closely, he would have seen his face on a poster. He was wanted for horse thieving and murder in The Nation.

* * *

We'd only been on the trail four days to get here, but Levi Noone and I were tying into the food at our favorite café like we'd just gotten off the trail from Tennessee again. Victoria watched while I buttered up my fourth roll.

"I cooked you guys dinner every night on the way here, you remember that, right?"

I looked up from my plate, feeling a little guilty. I remembered to chew and swallow before I said anything. "You did," I agreed, "and it was good food." I looked over at Levi. He was nodding his head up and down, but he didn't stop feeding his face.

"It's just..." I said, trying again. "It's just that we didn't get three squares a day, out there driving the cows and setting up camp and whatnot."

I looked over at Murph, who just shrugged. He'd decided to stay out of this, I guess. Victoria broke out into a laugh, and I relaxed.

"I'm just teasing," she said. "I'm glad to see you boys eat up. We did great on that cattle sale. Six dollars a head! Dad will be so pleased!" She reached into her bags and pushed ten dollars across the table to each of us. When we objected, she raised her hands. "He insisted! I can't ever go home if you boys don't take it." She laughed.

In the end, only Murph returned the money. He said he was just doing his job and couldn't take pay on the side as a Ranger. Victoria told me to use the money to buy another cow or two for the drive with Goodnight.

Levi tucked the money in his pocket, thanked Victoria, and left the table. "Got to step over to the sheriff's office and see about getting another job," he said.

Levi settled his hat on his head after he stepped out of the café and crossed the street to the sheriff's office. He took a step up to the boardwalk, then paused to let a lady pass in front of him. He looked left and right before stepping up to the Wanted posters on the wall. When he did, he caught a quick glimpse of a man turning the corner to walk down a side street.

Levi stared, then stepped up to the poster for Eli Perkins, hanging right in front of him. It confirmed what he'd thought just a second ago—it was the same man!

Hurrying down to the corner, his hand feeling for

his Colt, Levi rushed around the corner, staring up and down the street. The man was gone. Levi walked up and down the street, glancing into the shops as he went. Eli Perkins had vanished. Frustrated, Noone parked himself on a bench to see if Perkins came back this way. Two hours later, he gave up. Eli Perkins had slipped away from him.

\* \* \*

Victoria and I were back at the same café for breakfast the next morning. She had asked at the train station and found that her acting troupe had left by train for Ft. Worth the day before. She had time to catch them before they left for Denver, traveling by stagecoach. I didn't envy her about that. I'd seen those stagecoach seats. A big guy like me would have trouble fitting in.

Levi wasn't with us this morning. He had said something last night about a job, or someone he was tracking. We'd waited outside the café for a while, hoping he would show, but he hadn't come.

Victoria wanted to talk about how I could make a cattle drive with Goodnight. I said I would look for some cows to buy, then slapped myself on the forehead. "I could've just bought your cows!"

She grinned and reached across the table to pat my hand. "I'd already thought of that," she assured me. "But our cows wouldn't have been the best ones to buy. We had a mixed breed, and they wouldn't do that well on a long drive. You need longhorns, mostly. Those are trail cows. They can go forever without much food or water."

"Right," I said. I had heard that before, I'd just

forgotten. I looked out the window, thinking. "I could go down to the railroad station," I said. "Maybe I could buy some from somebody else bringing longhorns to the rail."

"I'll go with you," she said. Then she changed the subject. "You could go down to the telegraph office and send a message to Charles Goodnight," she said. "He might be in Ft. Worth. He spends some of his time there, right?"

I shook my head and grinned. "You're way ahead of me on all of this," I confessed. "Us moonshiners in Tennessee didn't have a telegraph office." I thought about that and confessed something else. "I have no idea how to send a telegram."

She patted my hand again. "I'll go with you for that, too."

Thirty minutes later, I was full of a mighty tasty breakfast. I put down my fork and reached into my pocket. "Why don't we get started?" I asked. "Maybe we could go down to the telegraph office first."

We left the café and started down the street, crossing to get to the telegraph office, which was just a couple shops down the street. When we reached the middle of the street, I heard a familiar voice.

"Nash Walker!" I knew that voice. I looked around behind me to see Shade Taylor standing in the middle of the street, hands at his hips, feet spread wide. "I've come for you!" he boomed.

\* \* \*

Levi Noone had skipped breakfast, as much as he loved a good breakfast, so he could observe from a distance the corner where he had seen Eli Perkins the day before. It wasn't much to go on, but it was all Levi had. There might be something about this corner that brought Perkins back. The one-hundred-dollar reward on his head would look good in his pocket.

Sipping on some coffee and munching on a biscuit, Levi kept watching for forty minutes. He kept his hat pulled low and got up to stroll around a few times. His patience paid off when Eli Perkins walked past him and continued on to a livery stable across the street and about thirty yards down from the café where Nash and Victoria had gone for breakfast.

Levi continued to pace back and forth, watching from the corner of his eyes, while Eli stopped and looked at the stable, tilting his head back to look up at the loft. Then he turned and walked away, stopping to talk to someone in the street before moving on.

Levi stared, then turned his attention back to the stable loft. His eyes swung over to the café, where he knew Nash and Victoria had gone. He knew he didn't have any time to lose. He trotted to the rail where he had tethered his horse and pulled his Winchester from the scabbard. Five minutes later, he was in the livery stable. An old man was snoring in the corner of the yard. Levi placed himself behind a haystack. He had a clear view of the loft and the street.

In another twenty minutes, he could see a murderous plan falling into place. Eli Perkins came to the stable, trotting past the sleeping old man and climbing into the loft. Out in the street, a man with double-tied-down guns was lounging against the wall of a shop two doors down from the café.

Levi could see what they were doing. He had to

hope it would be a fair fight out there in the street. He would take care of the ambush from the stable. Perkins had kneeled behind a hay bale in the loft. A rifle rested on the top of the bale.

The café door opened, and Nash Walker stepped out with Victoria. The stranger lounging against the wall stepped into the street and yelled. Up in the loft, Perkins moved the rifle slightly and crouched to sight down the barrel.

Levi was remembering the *Wanted* poster as he lifted his Winchester. "Dead or Alive," he mumbled to himself. As he laid the sights on Perkins's chest, he yelled, "Hey!" When Perkins swung the rifle toward him, Levi Noone pulled the trigger just once. He saw Perkins spill backward behind the hay bale as Levi's shot echoed through the livery stable.

\* \* \*

We stepped out of the café, moving toward the telegraph office. Victoria was holding on to my arm as we picked our way across the muddy street. Halfway there, I heard a familiar voice I hadn't really wanted to hear again.

It was Shade Taylor yelling my name, then I turned to see him standing in the street. I couldn't really make sense of what he yelled at me, but I knew what was going to happen when I saw him, braced and ready, in the street.

Victoria gasped and murmured something. She seemed to try to get in front of me. I pushed her back. "Get off the street," I yelled, watching Shade Taylor while she scrambled away.

As Victoria hurried over to the side of the street, one thing flashed through my mind. On that night when Murph and the Rangers had stopped the cattle rustling, Shade had drawn on me. I wasn't sure if his bullet had hit me or if it came from the man I killed, but either way, Shade didn't get in a fatal shot. I'd thought about it later. Maybe he had pulled that trigger just a little too soon. Maybe he would again.

The rest seemed to happen so fast, it was like moving through a dream. I heard a rifle shot from behind Shade, but I didn't dare peel my eyes away from him. I couldn't do anything about what was happening back there behind him.

He seemed to freeze for just a second, then his head moved back and forth ever so slightly. He came back to lock his eyes on me, but he hesitated for a second, watching me. Then his hand moved, and his pistol started up.

I had reached for my Colt just as soon as his eyes flashed and his hand moved. I cleared leather and came level, triggering a shot just as I felt a sting scorch across the side of my neck. My gun bucked in my hand, and I saw the shot drive him back.

His gun hand dropped, and he struggled to come level again. I stepped once to the side, then walked forward, firing twice. His gun went off into the dust as I moved toward him. Both of my shots went crashing into his chest. He staggered back, then went to his knees. He stared at me, and I could see his mouth opening and closing, but he was past saying anything.

Shade Taylor's gun fell from his hand as he landed on his back. I guess the blue sky of Texas was the last thing he saw. By the time I got to him, he was still staring up, but he wasn't seeing anything.

I dropped to my knees beside him, then a lot of confusing things happened. Victoria ran to me. She grabbed me and turned me a little, looking me over. I struggled to my feet.

"Your neck!" she burst out. "You're bleeding! Come away from him and sit down on the boardwalk!"

I started protesting, telling her I wasn't hit. My hand went to my neck and came away bloody, so I let her lead me over to the side of the street.

"Nash, sit down!" she insisted. "You've been hurt!"

I started shaking my head to say no, then I heard Murph's voice. "Better do what the lady says, Nash," Murphy told me. "Don't be a dang mule about this." Where had Murph come from? I wasn't sure.

I slipped down the side of a post to sit down. Levi Noone showed up from somewhere. I heard him tell Murph there was a dead man in the livery stable named Eli Perkins. He said they'd tried to set up an ambush.

Victoria had pressed a piece of cloth up to my neck. She was staring at the place where I'd felt the sting. "I think it's just a graze, honey," she told me. "I'm going to get the doctor."

I held onto her hand, not wanting her to leave. Murph turned to look at Levi Noone. "Get the doctor," he told Levi. "Doc Abrams. His office is around the corner and down two blocks." He pointed to show Levi the way.

"Not Doc Abrams," I whined. "I'm okay, don't fuss over me."

"What are you worried about?" Murph chuckled. "You know you're his favorite."

# Chapter 21
## *A Plan Comes Together*

They took me over to Doc Abram's office, that much I remember. Doc took a look at the place where my neck had sprung a leak, then went over to a cabinet, muttering to himself. He took out a nasty-lookin' needle and some thread, then he took out a big bandage.

"I hope you're only gonna use that bandage, Doc," I growled, "because my momma used to mend my socks with that other stuff you got out. No tellin' where you'd stick me with that thing."

He snorted and mumbled to himself some more, then came over and pulled away the cloth Victoria had put over the bullet crease in my neck. I growled again and shifted around on my cot. Victoria took my hand and told me to hold still.

After he bent over and spent a long time inspecting my neck, the doc finally put down the thread and needle and picked up the bandage. I heaved a sigh of relief, but that didn't last long. He poured something on my neck that burned like fire, and I had to grit my teeth and grab hold of the blanket.

Murph passed me a bottle under the blanket, and I had a good idea what it was. I took a good swig of it when Doc turned his back. I figure he could probably smell it anyway, and he knew what it was, but he didn't mind if it shut me up. Then he grabbed that needle to start patching me up, and I passed out.

The last thing I remember is Victoria telling Murph she was going down to the telegraph office after I went to sleep. I think I saw her sitting in a chair next to me when I came awake a couple of times during the night.

* * *

I looked around for Victoria when I came to in the morning, but I didn't see her. I couldn't be sure now if I had just imagined her in the chair last night.

Doc came in and poked around a little more, then pronounced himself satisfied with things when he was done. He told me I had to stay put for the rest of the day, and he would let me go tomorrow if things still looked okay.

Victoria came in with some breakfast from the café, then helped me to sit up and eat. Doc didn't seem to care what I was eating, so I helped myself to eggs, bacon, and coffee. The pain in my neck was easing up. I peeked underneath the blanket and saw that Murph's whiskey bottle was there and still half full. Victoria saw what I was looking at and took it away from me.

"Last night it was medicine," she told me. "Today, it's just whiskey. Maybe you can go over to the saloon with Murph and Levi when you're better and have a beer." She tucked the whiskey into her bag.

Murph breezed in and sat down about an hour

later. He filled me in on what had happened in the livery stable yesterday, just before Shade Taylor and I had our little dust-up in the street.

Victoria said she was going to the telegraph office. She gave me a kiss and handed something to Murph on her way out. I was pretty sure it was the whiskey. Murph waited until she left before he started telling me about things.

"A guy named Eli Perkins was an old saddle partner of Shade Taylor," Murph told me. "They had you all set up to get dry-gulched from the livery stable when Taylor braced you in the street. Perkins was up in the loft of the livery stable with his rifle, and he had a bead on you."

I stared while Murph reached over to pick up a cup and help himself to my coffee. "Levi Noone, your old buddy, had seen him the day before and had a poster on him. Dead or alive. Levi got into the stable before Perkins got there and called him out before Perkins could get off a shot."

"Levi shot him?" I croaked. I couldn't believe I had been that close to getting shot from ambush.

"Yep." Murph nodded and set the cup down. "Dead as Caesar. Levi done collected the reward."

Murph looked around for Doc Abrams, who was gone. He filled up a cup with some coffee for me, then produced the whiskey bottle from his pocket and poured a little into the coffee.

I grinned. "Victoria slipped the bottle to me when I came in," Murph explained. "Don't tell nobody I gave you this. Especially not the doc." He thought for a second. "Don't tell Victoria, neither."

I promised, and then we just sat and talked for a

while. Murph asked if I'd thought about being a Ranger. I told him I was thinking more about joining up with a cattle drive to get myself a stake.

Murph nodded. Victoria came in a couple minutes later, so Murph shook my hand and told me to look him up if I changed my mind.

Victoria took a seat in his chair. She sniffed my coffee, but I'd swigged it all down before she came. I don't think there was a drop left in there. She set the cup down and looked at me.

"Change your mind about what?" she asked. "What did Murph mean?"

I told her about Murph asking me to join the Rangers. She nodded and passed a piece of paper to me. "You'd make a good Ranger," she said. "But look at this first. It's the answer to a telegram I sent to Charles Goodnight yesterday."

I opened the page, then read it twice. I whistled and broke into a grin. "Wow!" I said. I read it one more time. Goodnight told me in the telegram that he was leaving from Ft. Worth in about two months on a drive to Denver over the Goodnight-Loving Trail. He had fifty head of cattle he would sell me if I wanted to make the drive with him. He told me where to find him in Ft. Worth.

Victoria watched me, smiling. "Will I see you in Denver?" she asked. "I'm taking the train to Ft. Worth to join the company."

"You bet!" I burst out. "I'll take the train to Ft. Worth with you!"

Her smile faded a little. She checked the clock on the wall. "I'm sorry," she said. "You can't. My train leaves in a half hour, then the stagecoaches leave for

Denver tomorrow." She got up and gave me a long kiss. "I'll see you in Denver, Nash," she whispered. Then she was gone.

* * *

Doc Abrams let me go the next morning. He said my neck was healing just fine. I walked out to the street and around the corner. I stopped and stared at the place where Shade Taylor had drawn down on me just two days ago. It seemed like a lot longer.

I shook my head and walked down to the café, where I ordered the same breakfast Victoria had brought to me yesterday. It seemed like it had tasted better then.

A shadow fell over the table, and I looked up to see a welcome face. It was Levi Noone. He pulled out a chair, sat down, and ordered some breakfast when the waiter came over to check on things. He sat and watched me eating for a moment, then leaned forward.

"I ran into Victoria on her way to the rail station yesterday," he told me. "She told me the doc would let you go this morning. You were already gone when I got to the doc's office. I figgered I could find you here. Too early for the saloon," he snickered.

He waited while they put his breakfast in front of him. "She told me you're headed for Ft. Worth, then Denver, gonna throw in with Charles Goodnight on a drive. Said you're going to buy some good trail cows from Goodnight."

"Yep. Sure am." I talked for a while about how I hoped to buy at a good price from Goodnight, then sell 'em for a profit in Denver. About fifty head," I said.

"After that, I'll come back to Texas and decide what's next for me."

Levi listened and nodded, looking out the window from time to time, then looking at me again while he ate breakfast. I ran out of words after a while. Levi leaned back and sipped his coffee, then set the cup down.

"The thing is," he said, "I'm kinda done with bounty hunting, I think. I haven't had to shoot but two people, but out there in the livery stable..." His voice trailed off. He cleared his throat and leaned forward. "Anyway, I was thinking," he said, "that maybe there'd be room for one more man on that drive. Think we could partner up?"

I grinned and reached my hand across the table. "Partners," I said. He shook my hand. "Partners again," he agreed. "From Tennessee to Texas to Colorado."

# A Look At

## Nash Walker: Trail to Denver
## (Nash Walker 2)

**He fought for a future in Texas. Now the trail to Denver may cost him everything.**

After staking his name with the Texas Rangers and falling for a captivating singer named Victoria, Nash Walker is ready to lay down roots. A chance at land—and a life worth living—comes when cattle baron Charles Goodnight offers him a place on a high-stakes drive along the Goodnight-Loving Trail. But the road to Denver is anything but safe.

While Nash rides with the herd, Victoria takes a perilous stagecoach journey through No Man's Land to join a Denver stage production. Unknown to them both, danger is closing in fast. A ruthless outlaw named Cole is shadowing the trail—set on bleeding the drive dry and making a deadly play in Denver.

Will the trail to Denver lead Nash Walker to everything he's dreamed of—or straight into a trap he won't escape?

### *AVAILABLE JANUARY 2026*

# About the Author

Patrick Lindsay came to Texas by way of Missouri, Canada, and California, and has been proud to call the Lone Star State his home for more than forty years now. He retired in 2017 from "another life" as a CPA, whereafter he turned his hand to writing.

He has read just about everything by Louis L'Amour and first decided to give Western writing a try on his initial day of retirement. He has been writing ever since and loves the idea that so many people get enjoyment from his work.

Patrick and his wife Michelle live on a cattle ranch near Fort Worth along with cows, horses, chickens, and a very spoiled Great Pyrenees dog. He is an avid fan of the St. Louis Cardinals and the Kansas City Chiefs.